PALMER GIRL

Dawn Klinge

Dawn Klinge/Genevieve Publishing
dawn.klinge@gmail.com
www.dawnklingecom

Publisher's Note: This is a work of fiction. Names, characters, places, and incidents are a product of the author's imagination. Locales and public names are sometimes used for atmospheric purposes. Any resemblance to actual people, living or dead, or to businesses, companies, events, institutions, or locales is completely coincidental.

Book Layout ©2017 BookDesignTemplates.com

Cover design by Evelynne Labelle of Carpe Librum Book Design.

Sorrento Girl/ Dawn Klinge. -- 1st ed.
ISBN 978-1-7346434-1-1

Dedication

To Derek, my husband and my biggest supporter

"For it is by grace you have been saved, through faith—and this is not from yourselves, it is the gift of God—not by works, so that no one can boast".

–Ephesians 2:8-9

CHAPTER ONE

It was too late to avoid being spotted. The last space on Elizabeth Nordeman's dance card was about to be filled. Taking one last discreet sip from her glass, she set it on the passing silver tray of a uniformed waiter. Then she turned and smiled politely at the elegant woman and the young man approaching her. They'd made a beeline toward her place at the base of the grand curving staircase where she'd paused to catch her breath after the last quadrille. She'd been hoping to make an early exit and return to her family's apartment upstairs without anyone noticing.

Drawing near was Bertha Palmer, their hostess, and judging by the determined look on her face, her motives were clear. Every high society woman of Chicago, minus the ones with marriageable daughters of their own, seemed united in her mother's cause, which was to introduce Elizabeth to every eligible bachelor of high social standing in the city.

Elizabeth sensed her mother watching the scene from across the Palmer House ballroom as if willing her daughter to make an effort and maintain her manners. So far this evening, she'd been dutiful, but this event was the last place she wanted to be at the moment.

"Mr. Harold Pierce, I'd like to introduce you to Miss Elizabeth Nordeman. Miss Nordeman recently arrived with her family from New York. Her father, Cornelius, is a colleague of your father's." Mrs. Palmer introduced the eager freckle-faced man at her side to Elizabeth in an efficient and breezy manner that was mixed with a trace of a southern drawl. "Miss Nordeman, Mr. Pierce, is a student at Northwestern University. I've known his family for years."

"How do you do, Mr. Pierce," Elizabeth said, giving a curtsy, then extending her hand.

"It's a pleasure to meet you." He kissed her hand. "May I request the pleasure of your company for this next dance?"

Mrs. Palmer excused herself and moved along to her next guests. Elizabeth, having no other option, accepted his offer and followed Mr. Pierce toward the dance floor. Under glittering chandeliers, hanging from a frescoed ceiling, men and women in opulent evening attire waltzed or milled about the edges of the room as an eighteen-piece orchestra played.

The waltz allowed Mr. Pierce the opportunity to pepper Elizabeth with unwelcome questions. He exercised a familiarity she was unaccustomed to from someone she'd just met. "What brings you to Chicago, Miss Nordeman?"

Ignoring his breach of etiquette, Elizabeth did her best to answer politely, while still focusing on the dance steps.

"The World's Columbian Exposition, sir," she answered.

"But that isn't happening until next year."

"Very true, sir, but my father works for the Exposition Corporation. There's much to be done before it opens." Elizabeth didn't elaborate any further on why her father left his insurance company, uprooted the family and brought them to live at the Palmer House for the next eighteen months. Anyone who read the papers already knew at least part of the story—or thought they did.

"Aha, I see. That's why Mrs. Palmer said our fathers were colleagues," Mr. Pierce said as he stepped on Elizabeth's toe. "My father is responsible for bringing the fair to Chicago."

An exaggerated boast. A great many people had contributed to the effort. Elizabeth merely nodded at the pretentious man.

The look of approval on her father's face as she waltzed past him was apparent, and it strengthened her resolve to please him. Even if it meant dancing with Harold Pierce. When the waltz ended, Mr. Pierce offered his right arm to Elizabeth and escorted her from the dance floor.

"May I offer you a refreshment, Miss Nordeman?"

"No, thank you." Elizabeth made a point of closing her fan, a sign most men in her circle would have understood to mean she wasn't interested in further conversation.

"I regret this evening's festivities are already coming to a close. Thank you for the honor of your company with the last dance. I will call on you tomorrow," Mr. Pierce said, being persistent.

"Thank you, sir, though I am not at liberty to accept that offer. You may ask my father." Elizabeth bowed her head toward Mr. Pierce, once again signaling the end of their conversation. At this, she turned on her heel, not waiting to hear Mr. Pierce's response. She was halfway up the stairs before she heard a loud voice call behind her.

"I'll do that!" Mr. Pierce called out.

Elizabeth kept walking, pretending not to hear, and let out a sigh. *Oh, dear, I hope I didn't encourage him.*

***

The breakfast room smelled like fresh coffee and bacon when Elizabeth joined her father the next morning. It was her favorite room in the apartment. Light poured in through the tall bay windows, and the sunny yellow floral-print draperies made the space feel cheerful. Patricia Nordeman always took her breakfast in bed, leaving father and daughter to themselves for the first meal of the day.

Glancing up from his newspaper, her father nodded, acknowledging her presence. "Did you sleep well, my dear?"

"Yes, Father." Elizabeth placed a napkin in her lap. "And you?"

"Good, good. You were introduced to Eugene Pierce's son, Harold, last night, I noticed. Nice fellow?"

"Pleasant enough, I guess, but I'm not interested in him if that's what you're hinting at. He might ask you if he can call on me. Please say no."

"No?" Cornelius frowned. "Elizabeth...his family has connections. We must be careful not to offend."

"Please?" She hesitated. "Enough with the matchmaking. I'll be careful. I promise."

Her father put down his paper with a sigh. "And what are your plans for today? More shopping?"

She had been thinking of going to Marshall Field's to see what was new, but her father's disapproval of that idea was communicated, clear enough, in the tone of his voice. Elizabeth came up with a new plan.

"Of course not, Father. I was going to take Sissy with me to the flower market. I wanted to put together some new arrangements for the apartment."

Since moving to Chicago, Elizabeth had been lonely. She missed Catherine, her best friend in New York. Though it wasn't proper to form friendships with the help, Sissy, her lady's maid, was the closest person she had to an ally in the city.

"Very well, but don't take the streetcar. Take the carriage. I'll tell Louis to get it ready for you."

***

Bertha Palmer and Elizabeth's mother, Patricia, were having tea in the Nordeman's apartment when Elizabeth and Sissy arrived home from the market that afternoon. An array of brilliant flowers, ferns, and grasses, wrapped in brown paper, weighed the women down as they walked past the front parlor. Peeking over the top of some yellow roses, Elizabeth smiled and greeted her mother and their visitor.

Mrs. Palmer, a tall, middle-aged beauty with sparkling blue eyes, laughed at the sight of Elizabeth's shopping haul. "I see you found the flower market, dear. I'm a patron of the Horticultural Society myself. The perfume from those packages is wonderful. As soon as you unburden yourself, please, join us. I would love to know how you're enjoying our fair city so far."

"Elizabeth, let Sissy take care of those. Please, come sit." With a dainty hand, her mother picked up the porcelain bell to ring for more tea. A picture of grace and refinement, Mother's afternoon tea gown matched the pink silk parlor chair she sat on. Elizabeth handed the flowers to Sissy, along with the feather-trimmed bonnet she was wearing.

"Sissy, please put them in water for now. I want to create a new centerpiece for the dining room. Oh, and make sure we have some fruit for the arrangement." She joined the other two women and sat on the settee.

"If you're interested in floral design, then you really must come to the garden show next week," Mrs. Palmer said.

"Elizabeth insists on creating all our indoor arrangements herself. She designed this piece right here," her mother said, gesturing with pride toward the display of pink chrysanthemums and ferns adorning the mantle.

"Well, it's quite beautiful, I must say!" Coming from Mrs. Palmer, this was a true compliment. Palmer House was a wedding gift from her husband, Potter, in 1871, and since then the hotel had become a grand and splendid part of Chicago's social life. Deeply involved in running Palmer House, she was responsible for many of its celebrated features, such as the elaborate floral arrangements displayed throughout the building.

"Thank you," said Elizabeth. "I would love to attend the flower show next week."

"Then you will come as my guest. I'll have my secretary send you the details." Mrs. Palmer took a sip of tea with an air of finality as if to say that settled the matter.

Elizabeth smiled gratefully. It was an honor to have an important lady like Mrs. Palmer take a particular interest in her well-being as a newcomer to the city.

"Before you arrived, Elizabeth, our guest was telling me about Harold Pierce." Her mother took a small cucumber sandwich from the tiered tray in front of her. "I know his family contributed a great deal to the upcoming exposition. Harold seems like a nice young man."

"Yes, I'm sure he is." Elizabeth said. Was there any way to change the subject?

Thankfully, Mrs. Palmer had other matters on her mind. She wanted to discuss the Women's Building, which would be a highlight of the Columbian Exposition and would feature exhibits that celebrated achievements from women across the world. Mrs. Palmer was on the board of directors.

Elizabeth listened with interest, silently hoping that Mrs. Palmer's feminist sensibilities might begin to influence her mother, who was more of a traditionalist. Mother's personal feelings on the topic at hand were hard to read, as she was a woman of unflagging composure. Her expression remained neutral, as always.

"It's time I must go," Mrs. Palmer said when the clock chimed on the hour. She stood and gazed at the floral arrangement on the mantel while she waited for the housekeeper, Annette, to gather her hat and gloves. "Miss Nordeman, I believe you have great talent. How would you like to create an arrangement for the lobby downstairs?" Elizabeth's face grew warm with pleasure. Before she could answer her approval, Bertha added, "Of course, you'll be paid a fair sum. We'll talk more."

"That's not necessary," Elizabeth's mother said, jumping into their exchange. "I'm sure Elizabeth would be delighted to offer her services as a favor."

Her mother walked into the vestibule with her guest toward the front door. Elizabeth understood her mother disapproved of the idea of her daughter working for pay. She didn't know whose will would prevail. Both Mrs. Nordeman and Mrs. Palmer were strong women.

When Elizabeth's mother walked back into the parlor, alone, she had a small purple box in her hands with a notecard. "A delivery for you," she said. "It was left at the door." Her left eyebrow arched with curiosity.

Elizabeth took the card and opened it. *This candy is sweet, like your smile. Let's talk soon. Harold.*

"It's from Harold Pierce," she said, not hiding her distaste for the man.

Her mother opened the box and frowned. Chocolates. They were beautiful but unwelcome. Such a gift was too forward. Elizabeth knew her mother thought so also. As far as she was aware, Harold hadn't even spoken to her father yet.

"They sure do things differently here." Her mother sniffed, a sign of her disapproval.

Elizabeth nodded. Her mother missed New York and their life there. Their apartment at the Palmer House consisted of many beautiful rooms, and it was exquisitely decorated in the most luxurious of furnishings. However, it was not comparable in scale or grandeur to the magnificent Fifth Avenue mansion the Nordemans had left behind.

"I'm going to go lie down before dinner. We're eating in tonight." Elizabeth's mother stopped, then lifted a chocolate from the box. "By the way, Mrs. Palmer would like a large floral arrangement for the front lobby delivered by Friday. She said to keep the receipts for reimbursement and add something for your labor."

Mrs. Palmer is a good influence on my mother. Elizabeth liked her—admired her, really. Her mother seemed tired today. Maybe that was why she hadn't put up her usual resistance. The steady stream of social activities hadn't stopped since they'd arrived last month. Every night they attended glittering parties, their grief masked behind beautiful clothes, a busy schedule, and good manners. Elizabeth was happy for a night at home. She hoped it would be just the three of them. Chicago was supposed to be a fresh start for her family and a chance to heal. Was it false hope to believe this could be possible?

CHAPTER TWO

E lizabeth was inspired. In the past week, since attending the flower show with Mrs. Palmer, the hotel had commissioned three more arrangements. Elizabeth enjoyed the diversion of creating flower arrangements—choosing just the right textures, color palette, and fragrance notes to enhance the Palmer's classic lines.

She also gained a secret pleasure from listening to hotel guests comment on her pieces. It was fun to have a secret. Her mother still had reservations about her daughter's engagement in any business activity, but she'd acquiesced with an understanding that Elizabeth would be discreet. Nobody but the Palmers, her parents, and a few staff members would know that the artist behind the exquisite floral displays gracing the Palmer House lobby was the Nordeman heiress.

A valet had just left the apartment with the last of Mrs. Palmer's orders that Elizabeth had been working on. The design she was just finishing held a profusion of pink and white roses in a lead glass Tiffany vase. It was meant for the front lobby desk. *Now what?* She could do something with the leftover roses and freesia. *Maybe a centerpiece for the sideboard in the apartment's breakfast room.*

Her father walked onto the balcony where Elizabeth was working and nodded approvingly when he saw what she was doing. He didn't say so, but Elizabeth could tell he was proud of her new venture. Cornelius cleared his throat, a habit that indicated his following words would include an unspoken request.

"Harold Pierce is persistent," he began. Tenacity was a quality Father admired. He was a self-made man who believed his great success in business was a result of nothing more than persistence and hard work. "Your mother will be home this afternoon. If Mr. Pierce calls on you today, there's no reason to send him away."

"You spoke with him?" A knot formed in the pit of Elizabeth's stomach.

"He came by my office yesterday to speak about you. Nice man."

Elizabeth frowned. "I thought we had an understanding.".

"And that was...?"

"I'm not interested in Harold Pierce."

"You danced with him one time! How could you possibly know if you were interested in him or not?" He furrowed his brow.

"Please, Father. I don't care for his manners, and I already have plans this afternoon."

"You don't need another afternoon of shopping, if that's what you were thinking. Your closets are already full of beautiful clothes."

It was true. Elizabeth enjoyed the attention she received for her sense of style and for always having the latest designs from Paris. She didn't need another dress right now, but still, she enjoyed walking along State Street, and Elizabeth liked to step into Marshall Field's, even if only for a quick peek.

She wanted to admire the show windows, touch the silks, and have a small piece of cake in the tearoom—anything to get out of the hotel and avoid Harold Pierce. But the sour expression on her father's face made Elizabeth change her approach. She looked at the rose in her hand. It gave her an idea.

"You know, Marshall Field's always has fresh flowers on display throughout their store. I was thinking—perhaps they could use my services. I want to take this arrangement over there and see what they think."

A smile played at the corner of her father's mouth. Because another quality he appreciated was initiative. "Yes, that's a great idea!"

Maybe he would forget about Harold Pierce, for now. Elizabeth picked up her scissors and snipped off part of a freesia stem. The sweet scent reminded her of strawberries. *If only there were a perfume as pretty as this flower.* She'd stop by the cosmetics counter at the store and see what they had— after she spoke with someone about the flowers.

When she looked up, Elizabeth saw her mother standing in the doorway.

"What idea would that be?" she asked.

"I was hoping someone at Marshall Field's would be interested in using my services as a floral designer. I made four dollars this week from the arrangements I sold to the Palmer House, but I want to do more. I like working with the flowers."

"Elizabeth, I'd hoped this was a passing fancy. It's not attractive for a woman of your standing to concern herself with *commerce.*" She whispered the last word as if it were dirty. "My goodness. You certainly don't need to. You have an eye for beauty and design, but really, you must know Mrs. Palmer's patronage is simply a courtesy because of who you are."

"Now, Patricia, I don't think that's true." Father's tone gave a hint of warning. His wife had gone too far.

"I won't use my name when I go into the store," Elizabeth said. "I'll acquire a job based on skill alone."

"You can try, my dear, but as often as you go to that store, I believe everyone there already knows who you are." Her father laughed. "We just dined with Marshall Field last week at the Pullman's house!"

This wasn't funny. Elizabeth wanted to believe Mrs. Palmer would have hired her even if her last name wasn't Nordeman. She would avoid Marshall Field at the store and talk to someone else about the job, if possible. She'd prove her parents wrong.

At least she'd dodged the discussion about gentlemen callers. The Nordeman name had brought Elizabeth plenty of suitors, but it was hard for her to know if their attention meant they cared about her—or her fortune. Ever since the fire, when she was left as the sole Nordeman heir, Elizabeth felt even more pressure. But she couldn't think about that now. Her father wanted her to marry someone who could take over his business. She wanted that too, but she also wanted to marry for love. And Elizabeth wanted to have her own role in the business. More than anything, she feared falling for someone who only wanted to marry her for her money.

Elizabeth admired her father because he'd made something of himself with hard work and determination. He grew up on a farm in poverty, but now he was the owner of the country's largest insurance company. While her mother was intent on downplaying that part of their history, Elizabeth loved it. Earning her own money this week, little as it was, had been exhilarating. She wanted to feel the same pride in herself that she was sure her father must feel about his accomplishments.

Mrs. Nordeman sighed, turned on her heel, and walked back toward her bedroom. "Take Sissy with you when you go."

***

The uniformed doorman, outfitted in green and gold, greeted Elizabeth and Sissy as they entered Marshall Field's. "Those are some beautiful flowers you have there, miss."

"Thank you." Elizabeth smiled appreciatively. "I'd like to speak to the person who's in charge of purchasing flowers for this store. Could you please direct me to the appropriate office?"

"You'll want to go up to the seventh floor and ask for Mr. Selfridge or Mr. Lewis," the man answered, studying Elizabeth, his curiosity apparent.

The two women moved past the cosmetics counters toward the grand staircase until Elizabeth stopped, placing her gloved hand on Sissy's arm. "Sissy, why don't you look around down here. Pick out a new parasol for yourself, and I'll pay for it. I'll be back in a few minutes."

Sissy complied, and Elizabeth continued toward the upstairs offices, hoping she wouldn't meet anyone she knew along the way. A woman wearing all black, just as the store girls on the floors below did, sat behind a desk at the end of a long hallway, gazing expectantly at Elizabeth when she approached. "May I help you, miss?"

"I'm here to see Mr. Selfridge. May I please speak to him?" She hoped she sounded more confident than she felt.

"He's not here right now," the woman answered. "And the flowers are for?" she asked, sounding curious.

"These are a sample. I make floral arrangements, and I wanted to see if Mr. Selfridge would be interested in purchasing some for the store."

"We have someone, in house, who does our flowers, but perhaps Mr. Lewis would be able to speak with you. He's in charge of visual merchandising. I'll see if he's available. Wait here." The woman headed toward a closed door across the hall before pausing and turning around. "I didn't get your name, Miss..."

"Nordeman. Elizabeth Nordeman." She watched the woman's face for a sign of recognition, but the lady simply nodded, and Elizabeth's shoulders relaxed. *Hopefully, Mr. Lewis won't know who I am, either.*

A few minutes later, the woman returned, followed by a tall, handsome, dark-haired gentleman. "Miss Nordeman, I'm John Lewis. What can I do for you today?" He gave a polite smile while motioning to Elizabeth to follow him back to his office.

The office was small and cluttered with boxes, stacks of papers, and old dress forms. Mr. Lewis moved some silk scarves off a chair, then pulled it out before offering it to her. Elizabeth glanced around the room. The sharp, well-dressed tall man in front of her was a surprising contradiction to the room he occupied. Mr. Lewis seemed young, not much older than her brother, Samuel, who had been twenty-three. What exactly did Mr. Lewis do as head of visual merchandising?

"Please excuse the mess." He made a casual gesture toward piled boxes. "I don't spend much time in this office. It's more of a storage closet, as you can see, because I do most of my work downstairs. I'm swamped right now, so I can only give you five minutes."

Elizabeth placed the vase of roses she'd been holding on the desk in front of her and offered what she hoped was her most charming smile. Then she explained the purpose of her visit.

When she finished speaking, Elizabeth exhaled. She'd been holding her breath, a habit when she was nervous. Elizabeth thought she saw a twinkle in his eye and a slight twitch at the corner of his mouth before he cleared his throat and looked down. She realized that he found this amusing, and it annoyed her. Then he turned and gazed from the window onto the street below, remaining quiet.

After what felt like at least a minute of silence, he nodded toward the vase on the desk. "How much would you charge for an arrangement like this?"

Elizabeth, more excited now, did her best to quickly estimate the cost of supplies in her head, adding a little extra for labor. "One dollar, sir, but this first one is free. And I'll need some vases."

"Can you have twenty delivered to the store by next Monday?"

Elizabeth's pulse raced. Was Mr. Lewis serious? Perhaps he was toying with her. Twenty arrangements? She thought about the small balcony off the front sitting room in her family's apartment at the Palmer House. She didn't have enough space! Her mother would undoubtedly disapprove. But there was no way she was going to turn down the job. "Of course, Mr. Lewis."

"Very well. Where shall I have the vases delivered to?"

"The Palmer House, sir."

John Lewis raised his eyebrows, but he didn't make any reference to the luxury hotel. "We pay upon delivery. Does that work for you?"

"Of course," Elizabeth said, pushing all thoughts of how she was going to accomplish this mammoth task out of her mind. She'd deal with that later. Elizabeth reached out to shake Mr. Lewis's hand. Instead, he took her hand, bowed slightly, and kissed it. Once again, she noticed a twinkle in his striking, deep blue eyes, and she quickly turned away.

When the meeting was over, Elizabeth went to find Sissy. She couldn't wait to tell her what had happened. "I'm not sure if Mr. Lewis thinks I'm up for the task, but he ordered twenty arrangements, and I'll show him I can do it" she said. Elizabeth couldn't get the idea out of her head that he'd somehow been teasing her the whole time. *Hopefully, I'm wrong.*

After Elizabeth purchased a new parasol for Sissy, they walked outside the store together to admire the new window displays.

"Who is Mr. Lewis?" asked Sissy.

"He's in charge of visual merchandising, though I'm not even sure what that means." She pulled on her gloves.

"It means, he's probably the person who created this beautiful display right there."

Elizabeth studied the scene in front of her. The dressmaker dummy in the window wore a sapphire silk evening gown by Worth. Thousands of delicate crystals hung from the ceiling, creating an effect of stars. Elizabeth could envision herself in the dress, dancing in a beautiful ballroom. Whoever designed this breathtaking window was an artist.

Mr. Lewis had given her a job, and for that, she was grateful. One thing she couldn't deny— the man was good at his job— if these were, indeed, his window displays. They were the talk of the town. People were always milling about the sidewalk outside the store and admiring the stunning displays.

CHAPTER THREE

*M*r. *Walters will appreciate these roses.* John Lewis moved the bouquet to the side of his desk. The maître d', only yesterday, had been complaining that the flowers in the tearoom were unacceptable. *I cannot display these drooping monstrosities*, were Walter's exact words.

When Miss Andrews told John a young woman was inquiring about a job as a florist that morning, John thought he'd dismiss her quickly and be on his way. Creating floral arrangements for the store was his responsibility, and he was quite capable. Walter was always complaining, and the tearoom flowers were not that bad.

John had to admit, Miss Nordeman's floral arrangement was superior to anything he'd ever created for the store, and her timing with the sample was perfect. He had more work than he could handle right now, and once again, would be at the store long after closing. His boss, Mr. Field, had been telling John to delegate more responsibilities and focus on what he did best, dressing the windows, but he'd also wanted fresh flowers throughout the store.

Seven floors of merchandise filled the huge building, so John could use help with such a monumental task. His job was to display it all in the most visually appealing way possible. Mr. Field wanted his store to be a palace, an entire shopping world in one place. He directed his staff to encourage customers to touch the merchandise and stay as long as they wished. He intended for them to experience shopping as a pleasure, which is why he'd added the tearoom, the library, and even a lady's lounge. Ladies came to the store not only to shop but to also socialize and relax— and Mr. Field was a rich man because of it.

Miss Nordeman's boldness surprised him. Her expensive clothing and mannerisms gave her away as a woman who'd probably never asked for a job before. The salesgirls who worked downstairs usually came from working-class families. They *needed* to work. Miss Nordeman obviously didn't.

Curiosity compelled John to listen to her sales pitch. Of course, he also had to admit—she was gorgeous. Her green eyes, dazzling smile, and fair skin flushed with a rosy glow had captivated him. What could it hurt to give the lady a chance? Twenty arrangements of flowers for the store would only cover about half of what he needed in a week, but even that seemed too large of an order for Miss Nordeman to successfully fulfill. He was baffled as to why she wanted the vases to be delivered to the Palmer House. Was she working out of a hotel room? Did she have help?

John gathered together some invoices he needed to drop off in accounting and picked up Miss Nordemans's roses so he could deliver them to the tearoom. He was leaving the office when Mr. Field came down the hallway toward him.

"I heard Miss Nordeman came up here this morning. What did she want?"

"She brought these," John said, holding out the flowers. "She wants to be our florist." He paused. Mr. Field seemed to already know Miss Nordeman. Of course, he recognized many of his customers by name. She was probably one of them. "Is Miss Nordeman someone I should already know?"

Mr. Field's expression of bewilderment gave John his answer. "Her father is Cornelius Nordeman of Nordeman Insurance. She's become one of our best customers since she moved here from New York. She wants to be our florist? Very strange. What did you say?"

"I ordered twenty arrangements for the store —to be delivered on Monday."

"Uh, huh. I don't have the slightest idea why Miss Nordeman would want or need to work as a florist for this store, but if the rest of the arrangements look as good as the one you have here, I won't get in the way. You, Mr. Lewis, better keep that lady happy. She's your responsibility now. Whatever it takes. Give the lady what she wants!"

Mr. Field walked away, leaving John to wonder if he had just gotten himself into a pickle. To save himself some work, had he just created a whole lot more? What if she was nothing more than a spoiled girl who was amusing herself at his expense? He needed a backup plan in case she didn't come through with the flower order next week.

***

The following Monday, John was in his office, sorting through fabric samples, and searching for colors and textures that would work for the new fall window displays when Miss Andrews opened his door and poked in her head. "Miss Nordeman is here, sir. She says she has your delivery waiting out front on State Street. She wants to know where to send the driver."

"Thank you, Miss Andrews. Would you please send a message downstairs to have Frank go outside and show the man around back?" John followed the secretary out of his office and found Miss Nordeman waiting to speak to him. She looked even prettier than he'd remembered. "Miss Nordeman, how do you do?"

She stood up. "Very well, sir. I've got your order downstairs, and I hope you'll be pleased."

"Wonderful. We can discuss what the store needs next and settle the account in a moment. But first, I'd like to see the flowers. Would you please accompany me to the loading bay where we receive our deliveries?"

Elizabeth smiled. "Yes, sir."

John enjoyed seeing the obvious delight on the florist's face as she followed him through the back rooms of the store.

"So, this is where the magic begins," she said.

He remembered feeling the same way when he'd first come to the store as a salesclerk, only five years ago. This area was loud, busy, and lacking in refinement, unlike the public areas of the store, but the space did have a certain appeal. Hundreds of containers were stacked in towers all around them. Workers unloaded wagons parked near the large open doors and shouted orders about which departments the crates were headed. As usual, the men were also crack-ing crude jokes back and forth—that is, until they saw a female in their presence. Women didn't usually come back here.

"Here we are," John said when he spotted some men taking carefully wrapped vases, full of flowers, from a wagon.

"I had to hire a wagon. The flowers wouldn't fit in the carriage." Miss Nordeman surveyed the vases, checking for any damage. Everything was perfect.

John nodded his approval. "I'm impressed, Miss Nordeman. Can you do this again next week?"

"Well sir, I'd like that—but I've run into a slight problem with production."

"What's that? How can I help?" John asked.

"I need more room to work." She looked around the cavernous space. "Is there a place here where I could arrange the flowers? I'll need a large table and a source of water."

The idea of having more opportunities to see Miss Nordeman was appealing, and Mr. Field *did* say to give the lady whatever she wanted. "I'll figure something out." "Come back tomor-row, and I'll have it arranged." John took the check he had in his front pocket and handed it to her. "Now, here's your payment for a job well done."

Miss Nordeman's face lit up with a bright smile. "Thank you, Mr. Lewis."

"It's John—you're welcome to call me John."

Miss Nordeman seemed uncomfortable, and she didn't say anything.

Oh, no...that wasn't appropriate. Why'd I have to go and say that?

A moment later, her expression relaxed. "Okay, John, then call me Elizabeth."

***

John thought about what Marshall Field had said earlier that day. *There's a gala benefit for the symphony at the Palmer House tonight. You should come with me. There will be important people there you need to meet.*

Mr. Field wasn't the easiest man to work for. He had high standards, along with a temper, and no employee wanted to fail at meeting his expectations. He was one of the most revered and influential businessmen in Chicago. So, when Mr. Field took a particular interest in mentoring one of his employees, it was both an honor and a burden. John appreciated the opportunities Mr. Field had been offering him, and he did his best to please his boss. That meant attending this gala, even though he sensed he would feel like a misfit among Chicago's elite.

Even though John knew he could play the part and could decently act the role of a successful businessman—inside, he still felt like a farm kid from Wisconsin, an imposter. This night was his first time inside the ballroom at the Palmer House. Enormous sparkling chandeliers, vaulted ceilings decorated with intricate frescoes, and a grand expanse of arched windows overlooking the city served as the backdrop for the glamorous crowd of well-dressed men and women who milled about the room. People were quietly chatting and drinking champagne as a sixteen-piece orchestra in the corner played a lively melody.

John examined the room, hoping that Elizabeth Nordeman might be in attendance. After all, she lived here, and these were her kind of people. He hadn't been able to stop thinking about her since their first meeting at the store. He'd never met such an enchanting woman before. Her confidence, her intelligence, and her sweet smile were just a few of the reasons John was drawn towards his new florist.

Elizabeth was coming down the staircase, on the arm of an older man, when John spotted her. Her dark blond curls were styled on top of her head, revealing the graceful line of her neck, and she wore a pink lace gown with puffy sleeves that emphasized her slender waist. John watched her greeting people with a smile. Would it be appropriate to approach her? The older man with her, must be her father, Cornelius.

Mr. Field, who was standing near, watched John and nodded toward the staircase. "Listen, son." He cleared his throat. "Your *florist's* mother came into the store today to talk to me. She asked for discretion in regard to her daughter's recent business venture. This..." Marshall hesitated then gestured toward the ballroom. "...is Miss Nordeman's world. Here, she's an American princess. And as much as I value entrepreneurship, such as Miss Nordeman has shown, not everyone does—especially when it comes to a young lady of her social standing."

"I understand, sir." The hors d'oeuvre John had just put in his mouth felt heavy, like lead, as he struggled to swallow it.

"And John, be careful." Mr. Field walked away, leaving John to wonder what he meant.

The dinner gong resonated through the room, and the crowd moved into the dining area to be seated. As John made his way toward the door, Miss Nordeman caught his eye from across the room. She nodded toward him and smiled.

She was seated at another table, making any conversation impossible.

Dinner was a long affair with seven courses. John tried to appear interested in what the young woman seated next to him had to say, but it was hard not to keep glancing toward the table where Miss Nordeman sat.

After dinner, when John was getting ready to leave, he saw Elizabeth once again, but this time she appeared to be deep in conversation with Harold Pierce, the pompous son of the banker, Stuart Pierce. The junior Pierce was a customer John had waited on when he was still working in the men's suit department. To his disappointment, Elizabeth didn't seem to notice John as he moved past.

Outside, rain drenched the streets. Mr. Field offered John a ride home in his carriage, but John declined, telling him his house was close by, and the walk would do him good. The downpour suited his current mood.

CHAPTER FOUR

It was the second anniversary of Samuel's death. September 13th, 1892, was an ordinary Tuesday for most people, but to the Nordeman family, a painful reminder that life would never be the same. Elizabeth's father went to his office, preferring to keep himself busy, but Elizabeth and her mother had chosen to observe the day by spending it together. They started by attending mass at Holy Name Cathedral.

After mass, mother and daughter walked, arm-in-arm along State Street toward the Palmer House. "Why don't we stop in at Marshall Field's, have some lunch, and do some shopping?" her mother suggested. She, much like her daughter, loved to shop.

"Yes, I like that idea." The past few weeks Elizabeth had been at the store often, but not upstairs, and not as a customer. She'd been spending long hours in the basement studio she shared with John Lewis, arranging flowers.

Elizabeth understood her mother missed her company now that she wasn't spending as much time at home. She'd begun to suspect that her mother's reservations, when it came to the floristry work, had more to do with a reluctance to share the time they were accustomed to having together than anything else.

Because of that, Elizabeth was on a mission today. She aimed to do her best to make her mother feel loved and maybe a little less lonely. As for her mother's grief, there was little Elizabeth could do, except to let her mother know she wasn't alone.

Outside the store, the ladies paused to admire a new window display. Two bicycles were leaning against a large artificial tree that John had made. Wax-covered autumn leaves were scattered around the base of the tree and hanging from the ceiling with nearly invisible wires. The leaves had been Elizabeth's contribution.

Mother studied the bicycles. "Did you know Bertha Palmer rides one of those crazy things around the city? She told me I should get one!" She laughed as if it was the most absurd suggestion ever, but something else in her expression told her daughter that she was also intrigued. It gave Elizabeth an idea.

"You know, they seem like fun! I've always wanted to try riding one..."

"You have? Oh, my. I'm afraid you'd break a bone!"

Elizabeth had planted the seed. For now, she'd smile and change the subject. "Come, let's go to the tearoom. I'm hungry."

The Nordeman ladies were seated at a small table by the window where they could chat and enjoy the view. They both ordered chicken pot pie, Samuel's favorite.

"Your brother used to sweet talk the cook into making him cinnamon & sugar pie crust chips with the leftover dough whenever she made pies. Remember that?"

How could Elizabeth forget? They'd both loved those chips. She'd once convinced her older brother, when they were little, to sneak into the kitchen after everyone in the house was asleep. She wanted to find the leftover chips and take them back to the nursery. When Nanny found the crumbs all over the bedsheets the following morning, she gave them both a scolding— until Samuel insisted that his sister had nothing to do with it, taking all the blame. He had to go without dessert for a whole week. He was always protecting her.

"I miss him every day." Elizabeth's eyes felt dangerously close to spilling a few tears. Guilt washed over her.

Her mother reached out and placed her hand on top of her daughter's, giving it a gentle squeeze. "I do too. Thank you for coming to mass with me today, Elizabeth. I'm glad we could spend this time together. Our lives were changed forever that day, and we'll always miss him. It pains me to see the way you're hurting. Nobody blames you. I wish you could forgive yourself."

Elizabeth knew her mother meant every word she'd just spoken, but the kindness felt undeserved, and it stung like salt in the wound. Wiping away a tear, as discreetly as possible, Elizabeth forced a smile. She didn't want to bring any more pain to her mother. Especially not today.

After lunch, Elizabeth took the long way to the shoe section so they could stop by the sporting goods department. The money she earned from the flowers was in her pocketbook, and she wanted to use the funds to buy her mother a gift. "Mother, look at this lovely red bicycle. What do you think?"

"What do I think? Well, I suppose it's lovely, but I thought we were going to see the shoes."

Elizabeth peered at the price. She could afford it. But should she?

"May I help you, Miss Nordeman?" a familiar voice asked behind her.

She turned to see John Lewis smiling at her, and her pulse quickened. Why did he make Elizabeth feel like she was some foolish schoolgirl with a crush? Her face warmed. She quickly regained her composure, knowing her mother was watching her.

"Mr. Lewis..." Elizabeth's mother would disapprove if she heard they were on a first-name basis. "Good afternoon. I was just browsing. I don't believe you've met my mother, Patricia Nordeman. Mother, this is John Lewis. He's the man responsible for the beautiful window displays downstairs, and I report to him for the store's flower orders."

"Mr. Lewis. How do you do? I admire your work." Her mother was cordial but somewhat cool toward John as they made polite small talk for a couple of minutes.

Mother noticed everything. Surely, she hadn't missed the blush that rose in Elizabeth's cheeks at the sight of John. Elizabeth felt some relief when he was called away by another customer and said goodbye to the ladies. Elizabeth wasn't ready to answer the inevitable questions her mother would be sure to ask about her relationship with window dresser. The less she had to go on, the better.

Later, after the Nordeman women had bought new shoes, Elizabeth thought about the bicycles again. *Yes, I'm going to buy that bicycle for Mother, and one for myself too.* They could go to the park and learn how to ride them together. It would bring some fun into their lives. Elizabeth hoped the surprise would not only delight her mother but also show her that she had no intention of letting her work come between the two of them.

While Patricia was speaking with a salesgirl at the cosmetics counter, Elizabeth quietly found John and gave him enough money to cover the cost of two bicycles, asking him to have them delivered to the Palmer House.

***

Elizabeth's hunch had been correct. Her mother loved the surprise. The happiness and pride Elizabeth felt when she saw her mother's face light up at the sight of two bicycles adorned with bright red bows was a memory she'd cherish.

The busy street in front of the Palmer House was unsuitable for practice, so Elizabeth and her mother had loaded up the new bicycles on the back of the carriage, and their driver had taken them to Lake Park, where there were fewer people to watch them fall.

Learning to ride a bicycle was easy for Elizabeth, but her mother was having a more difficult time. To her credit, she was trying her best, and even finding some humor in all of it. Only she couldn't seem to stay upright. Part of the problem was her extra-long skirt. It kept getting in the way—that, and fear. But it was a beautiful fall day, and in spite of a few minor crashes, Elizabeth was having a good time, and it seemed like Mother was too. .

"You need to pedal faster, or you'll just continue to tip over," Elizabeth said.

Her mother was currently wobbling along the pathway on her bicycle, but as soon as she started to pick up speed, she'd slow herself down again by dragging her feet.

"She's right, Patricia," a breezy voice called out. "You need to relax and enjoy the ride." Their friend, Bertha Palmer, happened to ride by at that moment. She got off her bike and leaned it against a tree.

"You rescued me, Bertha." Patricia laughed. "I think I need a break. What a pleasant surprise to run into you here.

"You'll catch on," Bertha said. "And once you do, it's the easiest thing in the world."

Bertha Palmer, even on a bicycle, was still decked out in her usual expensive jewelry. But instead of wearing a customary long skirt with a shirtwaist, she was wearing a shorter dress, and underneath, as one could plainly see, she had on bloomers. That was Mrs. Palmer—always glamorous but not afraid to take some risks.

The ladies found a bench and sat down together. Bertha pulled a tin of chocolate chip cookies out of the basket attached to the front of her bike and shared them. After a while, a cold breeze coming across the lake convinced the group it was time to get back on the bicycles. Louis, their driver, would be waiting with the carriage to take them home.

Elizabeth watched with satisfaction as her mother rode in front of her, doing much better than before. The wobbles had subsided, and her confidence seemed to be growing as she began to pedal faster. That feeling of pride began to change to concern as Elizabeth continued to watch. Her mother appeared to be going too quickly now, and she was losing control. A duck lazily walked across the path in front of them. Elizabeth watched in horror as the bicycle swerved sharply, then tipped over, dumping her mother swiftly to the ground.

"Mother! Are you all right?" Elizabeth shouted as she ran toward the scene of the accident. The bicycle was still on top of its victim. Her mother's face looked white with shock. Bertha, who had also run over, helped Elizabeth pull the bike off her mother.

"My wrist hurts. But other than that, I think I'm all right," her mother said, wincing as she got up. "Maybe I'm too old for this." Her elbow was bleeding and her skirt was torn.

"Oh, dear, accidents happen, but you're younger than I am, so let's have no talk about 'being too old' shall we? You avoided a crash with the ducks!" Mrs. Palmer said. "Let's get you home. I'll send for a doctor to come and have a look at your wrist."

A crowd of concerned bystanders was beginning to gather around the women. Elizabeth, knowing her mother disliked public spectacles, particularly when she was the center of one, quickly assured the crowd that all was well and put her arm around her mother protectively. "I'm going to ride ahead and get Louis so he can bring the carriage over here. Mrs. Palmer will stay with you until I get back. I'm so sorry this happened."

Elizabeth felt terrible. Guilt washed over her as she rode as fast as she could to get Louis. Guilt—as if there wasn't already enough of it. Hopefully, her mother's wrist wasn't broken, but based on its odd angle at the moment, she guessed it was. And what if something worse had happened? The thought made her shudder. Elizabeth wanted to feel free from the burden she'd been carrying since the terrible night of the fire.

Her unhappiness is my fault, and now I'm the cause of this. Why did I get her a bicycle? What's wrong with me?

For a while, when her mother had been smiling and laughing that morning, Elizabeth had felt lighter. But now, all the old feelings returned. She'd never be able to atone for all the pain she'd caused her parents—even if she spent the rest of her life trying. If only she'd listened to them. If she had, Samuel would still be here today.

CHAPTER FIVE

J ohn watched as Stuart Peterson, one of the delivery drivers for the store, carried a large box into his work studio. "Is the *Palmer Girl* still around? I have the vases she requested for the tables in the tearoom." Stuart and many of the other men who worked in the loading bay had affectionately adopted the name, Palmer Girl, for Elizabeth.

Even though she now operated out of the basement studio at the store, the story of how she'd, at first set up shop in her luxurious Palmer House apartment still amused the men to no end. They'd all assumed the penthouse princess would quickly grow bored and abandon the job. But instead, she'd proven them wrong and earned their respect. Not only was she good at what she did, but she was reliable and committed to keeping the store supplied with fresh flowers, week after week.

"No, she's gone for the day. You can leave that on the table over there. I'll make sure she gets it," John said.

Stuart seated himself on a bench and took a cheese sandwich, wrapped in wax paper, from a coat pocket. "You hungry? Take half," he said, offering some to John.

John gratefully accepted. He'd worked straight through lunchtime. Even with Elizabeth's help on the flowers, there was still a pile of work threatening to bury him. Though, if he was honest, he'd been somewhat distracted lately. Working closely with Elizabeth wasn't as easy as he thought it would be. Instead of focusing on the tasks at hand, too often, John found himself focusing on the beautiful florist who shared a studio with him. She was more than just a lovely woman, however. Her kindness, the tender way she handled the plants, and her strong work ethic were all deeply attractive to him. And John was starting to depend on her, which wasn't a position he wanted to put himself in. He needed a slap upside the head—something to get him thinking straight again. Elizabeth Nordeman wasn't someone he could afford to have feelings for. They were from two different worlds.

"There's this salesgirl, up in cosmetics—her name's Matilda," Stuart said. "I want to get to know her better. I thought it might be fun to go out after work and have dinner together, but I need your help. She won't come if it's just the two of us. Why don't you come, too, John? I'll invite my sister, Mary. She works in cosmetics with Matilda. It'll be fun!"

Is Stuart trying to play matchmaker between his sister and me? It didn't matter. John needed a distraction. Mary seemed like a nice girl—and pretty too.

"All right then, sounds like a plan," John said. "Come find me at the end of the day, and I'll tag along. But for now, you need to get out of here. I've got to finish these plans I'm drawing up for the new toy department."

A nine-story annex to the store was now under construction. Mr. Field wanted it finished before next year's Columbian Exposition. The toy department was only one of many new areas that John was responsible for furnishing.

John worked steadily throughout the rest of the afternoon. He was anticipating an evening out with friends. Usually, John worked long after the store closed. There were so many parts to his job that he couldn't do when customers were around. As lonely as it could be, John couldn't complain. He loved his career, and he loved living in Chicago. He'd worked hard to get where he was—the plan being to follow in Gordon Selfridge's footsteps and continue advancing at the store until he made partner.

Gordon Selfridge, much like John, started from nothing, but Marshall Field had seen promise in him. Now, see where the man had arrived—married to Rose Buckingham, living in Hyde Park, and a junior partner at the finest department store in Chicago. Did his boss see the same promise in him? If he was as successful as Mr. Selfridge, then maybe, he might stand a chance with someone like Elizbeth Nordeman. But he still had a long way to go. John was lost in these thoughts when Stuart knocked on his door.

"Hey, John. You ready? The ladies are waiting upstairs."

John stood, grabbed his coat from the hook on the wall, and turned off the lamp. "I'm ready. Let's go."

Mary Peterson and Matilda Mathews had both changed out of the black dresses used for work. Mary was attired in a fashionable green suit with a high lace collar. A matching hat topped the curly red hair piled on top of her head. Matilda wore a similar suit but in pink. John was acquainted with both women but had always viewed them strictly as coworkers. Seeing them both now, dressed up for a night out, caught him off guard. Maybe he should have changed into something more appropriate.

"Good evening, Miss Peterson. Miss Mathews," John said.

"Ladies, what do you say we go to Bailey's on Wabash Ave? They should have live music tonight," Stuart said. Then he whispered to John, "Isn't Matilda pretty?"

John smiled and offered his arm to Mary. Stuart did the same for Matilda. Yes, both of the girls were attractive. The group left through the front entrance onto State Street. Bailey's was near enough to walk, and Mary stuck close to John. He assumed it was due to the chilly evening. Actually, she was practically hugging his arm.

They arrived at the restaurant and were seated. Mary took off her gloves and hat and placed them on the table. She looked at John and smiled, then put her right forefinger to her left eye. Matilda, who was watching, gave a knowing laugh. It must have been some code between the women, but John didn't know what it meant. Mary repeated the action a couple more times before finally picking up her menu.

John, now feeling slightly uncomfortable, studied his menu before finally deciding on the steak. Mary was a sweet girl, but she seemed to be flirting with him, and he didn't want to give her the wrong idea. The rest of the evening, he did his best to remain polite but cool. It would be wrong to use Mary as a distraction from Elizabeth.

***

"I'm going to New York next week, and I'll be gone for fourteen days," Elizabeth said.

John swept some leaf clippings off the workbench and into a garbage can, nodding. They were in the downstairs work studio. Buckets of roses, greenery, and heather filled the small space, scenting the air with sweetness. "That's fine. I'll find someone to fill in for you while you're gone. Any special plans while you're there?" He tried to sound calm, but inside, John was feeling anxious. Together, they made a strong team. He needed her at the store. And frankly, he'd miss her.

"I'm going to visit my best friend, Catherine. I haven't seen her since I came out here. We'll probably do some horseback riding, maybe some sailing, go for long walks, that sort of thing. She has the most beautiful place in the country."

"That sounds nice." John thought about his family's farm in Wisconsin. It had been more than a year since he'd last visited, and though he didn't miss farm life, he did miss his family.

"You know, I usually go to the flower market on Mondays. Since I'm not leaving until Tuesday, I could still go and bring back a good supply of stock to work with— if that would make things easier."

John appreciated her thoughtfulness. Elizabeth seemed to know exactly which sellers to buy from, and she had a special knack for getting the best from them. When John went to the market, he seemed to end up with roses that wilted and dropped their heads in less than a couple of days. "What if I came with you this time? You could introduce me to your vendors. I need to learn your secrets."

"Okay. I'll see you on Monday morning. I'll come to the store first, and we can leave from here. As for now..." Elizabeth glanced around the room, checking the arrangements she'd done so far. "I think I need to put some of these bouquets on a tray and send them upstairs on the dumbwaiter—make some room so I can get the rest done."

***

John was happy to find Elizabeth in his office that next Monday. "Are you ready?" she asked.

John scooped up his bowler hat and overcoat. "Sure am—ready to learn." Together, they walked downstairs. As they moved through the cosmetics department, on the way out the door,

Mary Peterson looked up from the powders she was arranging on the counter.

"Mr. Lewis, Miss Nordeman—good day. Where are you two off to?" Her tone was high pitched and taut.

"Good morning, Miss Peterson. We're just going out for an errand." John ignored the scowl that came over Mary's face.

Elizabeth had a carriage waiting on State Street, in front of the store. Have you always lived in Chicago, John?" she asked once they were on their way.

"No, I've been here for about five years now. I'm from the Belmont area of Wisconsin. I grew up on a farm. My folks still live there, though my brother, Horace, runs the farm now."

"What brought you to Chicago?"

"I came here to study at the Art Institute. But to pay the bills, I started working at the whole-sale store over on Franklin. When Mr. Field asked me to come over to the department store and head up visual merchandising, I couldn't pass up the opportunity. I still like to paint when I can, but there isn't a lot of time left over at the end of the day. John relaxed against his seat back. What about you, Elizabeth? What brought you to Chicago?"

"We lost our home a couple of years ago in a fire. It's being rebuilt, but it will take some time. My father has a longstanding friendship with Potter Palmer, and when Mr. Palmer asked him to serve as an advisor on the Exposition Corporation, he accepted the position and brought my mother and me to live in the nation's only fireproof hotel."

John nodded. The first Palmer House Hotel was destroyed in the Chicago Fire, only weeks after its completion. Elizabeth lived in the second version—a place just as grand as the first, but now, widely touted for its fireproof rooms.

"I'm sorry to hear about your home. I can only imagine how hard that must have been," he said. The more John learned about Elizabeth, the stronger his admiration and respect for her grew. She had a quiet strength and depth of character that attracted him to her.

They arrived at the flower market, and the place was already bustling with activity. Cramped, dark stalls filled a large, low-ceilinged warehouse. If not for the beauty of the flowers, the market would have been an ugly place.

Though petite, Elizabeth had no problem maneuvering her way through the crowds. She confidently bargained with the vendors, securing the healthiest flowers at the best prices. John was impressed.

"I hope I'm not revealing all my secrets—only to be out of a job, Mr. Lewis!" Elizabeth said with a smile.

"Never. I expect to see you back here in two weeks." John counted himself lucky that this sweet woman who'd shown up at his office a month ago was someone he got to work with.

The jovial atmosphere dissipated suddenly, however, when a loud crash somewhere behind them jolted Elizabeth. Her eyes widened with terror. An oil lamp in one of the stalls had fallen over, setting a nearby table on fire. The vendor quickly grabbed a metal bucket, dumped the flowers out, and smothered the flames by covering them with the bucket. The smell of smoke quickly filled the air.

Elizabeth picked up her skirt and ran to the carriage. When John caught up to her, Elizabeth's face was white, and she was shaking. The confident woman she'd been, minutes before, was gone.

"The fire is out. It's okay," he said.

"I'm ready to go home now." Tears filled her eyes.

John offered Elizabeth his handkerchief. How awful it must have been for her to have lost her house in a fire. Softly, he asked, "Elizabeth, do you want to talk about the house fire?"

"No, not now," she whispered.

CHAPTER SIX

A t Grand Central Station, Elizabeth and her mother said goodbye to each other. They'd traveled to New York together in their private train car. Sissy and Annette, their servants, had accompanied them. Here, they were going their separate ways. Mother and Annette would be spending the next few days in the city at The Plaza Hotel. Elizabeth's mother needed to meet with her architect and designer, and she had a lot of furniture shopping to do. Their home on Fifth Avenue was nothing but an empty shell at the moment. Mother was determined to rebuild and to make it even better than it was before.

Elizabeth would rejoin her mother in a few days. But first, she and Sissy had another train to catch. They were headed upstate to Port Chester, a small seaport village north of the city. Elizabeth's friend, Catherine, lived there.

Happy memories of long summer days reading novels, horseback riding, and spending time in the gardens talking with her friend filled Elizabeth with excitement over returning to these simple pleasures. She'd spent a lot of time at the

Rosen Estate, Catherine's family home, during school breaks over the years. Now, Catherine was married, and Elizabeth would be staying at Davenport Manor. Though Elizabeth had never been inside the grand house where Catherine lived with her husband, she was acquainted with its exterior.

For as long as Elizabeth could remember, her friend was infatuated with Harry Davenport, the boy who lived there. The girls used to ride their horses nearby, always hoping to catch a glimpse of Harry. Catherine's infatuation eventually turned to love. Happily, it was one that was reciprocated, and Elizabeth was able to witness the couple's wedding vows shortly before she left for Chicago. It was a beautiful wedding—one that gave Elizabeth hope for a love story of her own.

Elizabeth couldn't wait to join Catherine, whom she hadn't seen in six months. It would be just the two of them this week, like old times. Harry was traveling on business, and the timing couldn't have been more perfect. It wasn't that Elizabeth didn't want to see him—she was just excited to have Catherine all to herself.

The ride to Port Chester was over in a few hours—nothing like the long trip from Chicago. Elizabeth spotted Catherine waiting on the platform when the train pulled into the station. Upon exiting the train, Elizabeth ran to her friend, forgetting any sense of decorum.

Catherine, who was tall, slender, and blond, appeared more beautiful than ever. If she wasn't one of the kindest people Elizabeth knew, she might have been jealous, but that was impossible. They'd been close since the age of ten. An instant bond had formed when they'd been placed together as roommates at Mrs. Okill's Academy.

Today, Catherine was wearing a delicate seafoam green tea gown with a straw hat. Her overcoat was thrown across her arm, for the afternoon sun was unusually warm this fall day. She looked elegant and cool. Elizabeth, who was wearing a stiff wool traveling suit, felt perspiration dripping down her back. She was glad the carriage ride to Davenport Manor would be short, as she was anxious to change into a dress more like what Catherine was wearing.

"You're right on time, Lizzy!" Catherine, who was the only person allowed to use that nickname, gave Elizabeth a mock look of amazement. "How are you, my sweet friend?" she said as she gave her Elizabeth a hug.

"Mrs. Davenport, I'm happy to be here!" Elizabeth stood back and adjusted Catherine's hat. "Marriage obviously suits you. It's good to see you! And what would make you think I'd be late?" She smiled and gave a wink. Being tardy for just about everything was a habit of Elizabeth's—something Catherine endlessly teased her for—all in fun.

"And Sissy, it's wonderful to see you again," Catherine said. "How was the trip?"

"Uneventful, Mrs. Davenport, just the way I prefer. It's good to see you too," Elizabeth's maid said.

Catherine smiled, wrapped her arm through the crook of Elizabeth's, and began leading the ladies toward the waiting carriage. "We have just enough time to go home and change for dinner. On the way, I want to hear all about this flower business of yours that you mentioned in your letter."

The women caught up on the news from their lives as the carriage moved past bucolic farms on one side of the road and seaside views on the other. The scent of freshly cut hay mingled with the salty air. Elizabeth relaxed into her seat and enjoyed the muffled sound of the two horses' hooves on the soft dirt road.

Catherine pointed to a church that looked like a castle, complete with turrets. "I've been playing the piano at Summerfield on Sunday mornings."

"It's beautiful. Everything feels so peaceful here," Elizabeth said. "I can't wait to hear you play."

The carriage stopped, and Elizabeth stepped out and admired Catherine's lovely home. The red brick mansion was stately. Its twelve over-sized windows were perfectly aligned, three on each side of the large white doors, on each of the two levels. A graceful balcony, situated directly over the doors on the second level, looked out over the vast green lawn, and farther beyond, one could see the waterfront.

"Madam Davenport. Miss Nordeman. Welcome," a tall uniformed butler said as Elizabeth followed Catherine inside.

Elizabeth's first view was of a large curved staircase with a dark wood banister. To the right, a wide doorway led to a light-filled parlor. Catherine's grand piano was in the corner.

"I'll show you to your rooms," Catherine said, leading the way up the stairs. "Dinner is at seven. It will be just us tonight, but tomorrow I'm throwing you a welcome party. It will just be a few neighbors, my parents—who can't wait to see you—and Harry's parents, who recently came back from Europe. They're living in the cottage on the edge of the property."

Elizabeth had seen the cottage on the way in. It was nearly as large as the main house.

***

After church on Sunday, Elizabeth and Catherine decided to take advantage of the warm day and walk back to the house. Six days at Davenport Manor had been precisely what Elizabeth needed. She'd enjoyed every moment with her friend and was sorry that she'd need to say goodbye the following day. No one else knew Elizabeth as well as Catherine. It seemed as if she could read Elizabeth's mind at times.

"You played the piano beautifully this morning." Elizabeth opened her lace parasol. "I loved how you performed 'Amazing Grace.'"

"'Twas grace that taught my heart to fear, and grace my fears relieved.'" Catherine quoted the words from the song slowly. "Those are some comforting words."

Elizabeth remained quiet. She stopped to pick some black-eyed Susans growing on the side of the path. "Yes, sometimes I have a hard time believing there's any truth behind them, though. There are times when I start to feel happy again, but then something happens to remind me of that awful night when Samuel died. The weight of it is crushing. I don't deserve grace. I'll never stop regretting what I did."

"I can see why you might feel that way, even though I believe you're too hard on yourself. But nobody deserves grace. That's the whole point." Catherine placed her hand over her friend's. "You know you don't have to go back to Chicago. You're welcome to live with Harry and me until your new house is finished. You always have a home here."

"You're very kind. Thank you. I love it here. I really do, and I love being with you. It was lonely when I first arrived in Chicago, not knowing anyone, but it's getting better, and my parents need me. I couldn't leave them right now." She hesitated. "Or maybe—on second thought, they are trying to get rid of me." She paused and smiled. "They've been arranging introductions between every eligible wealthy man in Chicago and me. Nonstop. It has been refreshing to have a break from all that pressure. But I do enjoy the floral design work I've been doing, and I promised John I'd be back."

"Who's John?"

"Oh—John Lewis. He's in charge of visual merchandising at Marshall Field's. We share a work studio. He designs the most beautiful window displays. People often come to the store just to see them."

"Aha." Catherine gave a knowing smile. "Tell me more about John."

Elizabeth wanted to protest. She knew what her friend was thinking, and she wanted to correct her, but doing so would only encourage Catherine to ask more questions—something she wanted to avoid. Elizabeth hadn't meant to sound so enthusiastic. *Catherine thinks I have feelings for John? Ridiculous.* "He gave me a chance. That's all. He's my client. I just want to prove to myself that I'm good for more than shopping, attending balls, and finding a husband who can take over my father's business. Now, I'm running my own business."

"Elizabeth, dear, I'm proud of you, and you've always been good for a whole lot more than those things you mentioned. But, if you're enjoying the work, then keep at it. This man—John—he sounds like a good person," Catherine said as she gave Elizabeth a playful nudge and winked.

***

A week later, back in Chicago, the Nordemans were having dinner together, discussing plans for the new house, and listening to each other's stories from their time apart. Then the conversation took an unpleasant turn.

"Elizabeth, darling," her mother said, "I had tea with Mrs. Harris today, and she brought something to my attention that has me concerned."

Elizabeth wasn't sure who Mrs. Harris was, but something in her mother's tone told her this concern had something to do with her.

"She said you were seen taking a carriage and walking around the flower market—accompanied by an unknown man—shortly before we went to New York. She asked if you had recently become engaged." Patricia paused. "Elizabeth, who was he?"

Frustrated and annoyed, Elizabeth nearly choked on a piece of bread she'd just taken. Taking a sip of water, she composed herself. "That would be Mr. Lewis, from the store. I was introducing him to some of the vendors I buy from so he could continue supplying the store with flowers while I was away. He's a gentleman. There was nothing improper about the outing."

"It's inappropriate, as you well know, and I have it in mind to put a stop to this flower business, once and for all."

Elizabeth's father put his fork down and cleared his throat. "Now Patricia, let's not get carried away." He turned to Elizabeth. "Promise your mother there will be no more of this. I don't need to remind you that people talk—and whether you like it or not, you have certain responsibilities to uphold as part of this family. You can't be too cautious with your reputation."

"Yes, Father," Elizabeth said. "Mother, it won't happen again. I'm sorry my actions put you in that position with Mrs. Harris today." She was disappointed in herself.

CHAPTER SEVEN

J ohn's meeting with the architect, Mr. Burnham, along with Mr. Field and Mr. Selfridge
had lasted all morning, going longer than
expected. They'd been discussing plans for the
new addition to the store. The goal was to have it
open within the next few months—just in time
for the World's Fair. Though it was hard to believe they'd be ready in time, John sensed it was
going to be truly spectacular. It was exciting to
be a part of such an important project.

It was two o'clock already. John was trying to
make his way from the upstairs offices back
down to his basement studio as quickly as possible. Elizabeth said she'd return today, and he
was hoping to see her while she was still around.
When she came into the studio to work, she
usually left around two.

There were eight flights of stairs at the store,
and on each floor, employees who wanted to talk
to him and ask questions. He was slightly out of
breath by the time he reached the hallway outside his studio at ten past two. Slowing down, he
straightened his tie and turned into the open
doorway. Hope turned to disappointment as he

looked around. A faint scent of roses perfumed the air, indicating the florist had already been there and left.

Annoyed, John pushed a couple of crates containing props out of the way with his foot. He didn't have time to be hanging about the studio anyhow. Several new shipments of ready-to-wear-dresses still sat in boxes over in receiving. Those needed his attention before they could be sent upstairs with instructions for the salesclerks on how to display them. He was losing his focus. It was time to think about work.

First, he needed something to eat. Hunger was gnawing at him and it was nearly two o'clock already. John regretted turning down an invitation to go to Mr. Field's club for lunch today—and for no good reason, either. He'd claimed he had too much to catch up on in the office, but the truth was, John wanted to see Elizabeth. He'd missed seeing her around the store over the past couple of weeks.

With two departments to reset after closing, dinner would, once again, be a can of baked beans heated over the stove and a slice of buttered bread—alone. At first, when he'd moved to Chicago, he'd enjoyed living by himself. It was a big change from life with a large family in a small farmhouse. But lately, he'd found himself avoiding his empty apartment as much as possible. He missed the laughter around the dinner table that he'd taken for granted growing up. Working long hours at the store was preferable to being alone. At least there were people around.

John unwrapped a piece of dried meat he'd stashed in his pocket and took a bite, trying not to think about the beautiful florist. He glanced to his right and noticed a red tin on the workbench. A folded paper sat on top with his name printed in neat letters. He unfolded the paper and read the message.

John,

I'm sorry I missed you today. I delivered all the flowers to their appropriate departments. Enjoy the fudge, a little souvenir from New York.

Cordially, Elizabeth

The delicious fudge almost melted in his mouth. John smiled to himself. Elizabeth had been on his mind often over the past couple of weeks. What did a gift like this mean? Had she been thinking of him, also? The small glimmer of hope he'd been holding sparked brighter.

After finishing his lunch, John decided to take a peek at the clothing that had recently arrived. He pried the lid off the first crate. It wasn't ready-to-wear like he'd thought. Several bolts of white silk were tucked inside. That's right. Mr. Selfridge had requested a window display with a wedding dress as the centerpiece. Mrs. Sanders, the store's head seamstress, had been asking when the silk she needed was going to arrive. John would deliver the fabric to her personally.

Two floors up, in the alterations department, his favorite seamstress greeted John. "Thank you, Mr. Lewis. I best get straight to work on this dress. You need it at the beginning of January, right?" Mrs. Sanders scrutinized the silk as she held it in her hands. "It's exceptional quality, sir. Do you already have a plan for the window?"

"Yes, I'll need it then. Here's what I was thinking for the dress." John handed her a sketch. "I'm on the search for a stain-glassed window I can use as a backdrop behind the dress, something to evoke the feeling of being in a church. I'll probably use fresh flowers too."

"This design is beautiful, but it won't be easy." Mrs. Sanders was summoned to help another customer just then. She waved her hand in the air as she walked away. "Don't worry, Mr. Lewis. We'll make it happen. I'll need another seamstress, though."

"You got it."

John went up to the seventh floor to put in a request for another seamstress. The thought occurred to him, for at least the third time that day, that he was going to appreciate the addition of elevators to the store. They couldn't come soon enough.

As John walked home after work that evening, he passed the Palmer House Hotel. When would he see Elizabeth again? Other than the store, and the one time at the gala, their lives rarely intersected. *What can I do to change that?* As he continued his route, he passed Holy Name Cathedral. He was admiring the building and the magnificent bronze doors when he was reminded of something—Elizabeth had mentioned this was where she attended mass.

John hadn't been to mass in a long while, despite the reminders his mother included in nearly every letter she sent. Sundays were his only day off from work, but maybe it would be worthwhile. He could make his mother happy and maybe run into Elizabeth Nordeman at the same time. *Yes, that's what I'll do. I'll go to mass.*

***

Sunday morning dawned bright and cold. John could see puffs of breath in the air when he woke. Getting out from beneath the warm covers wasn't easy, but the thought of possibly seeing Elizabeth encouraged him to make the necessary effort.

Sunlight spilled through the solitary window in John's studio apartment, highlighting its state of disarray. He needed to hire someone to come in and clean the place. He'd tried to keep up with it himself and save every penny for the home he hoped to build someday. But when it came to tidying up, John preferred painting in the few spare hours he had outside of working at the store. Besides, nobody ever saw his place.

A quick breakfast of coffee and toast, a hot bath, and a clean suit was all John needed to feel more awake and ready for church. He hadn't meant to neglect it, or God, for so long.

Part of John had wanted to wait until success happened. However, what had started as a goal to succeed artistically had morphed into something new—a desire for prosperity in business. It was taking longer than he'd expected. John didn't feel particularly successful at anything right now. Sure, he was receiving some attention for his window displays, but he was still a long way from having the wealth and respect he wanted.

On trips home to Wisconsin, John often felt ashamed at his lack of progress, and his feelings weren't any different when thinking about how God must see him. He wanted to have something to show for all his hard work. It would happen. John knew. He would achieve his goals. John just hoped success would happen soon, as he found himself wondering, more and more, if God was bringing him and Elizabeth together.

The cathedral was a short fifteen-minute walk from John's apartment on Wabash Ave. Five minutes into his journey, John heard a familiar voice behind him, and he turned.

"Mr. Lewis, good morning!" Stuart Peterson called out. His sister, Mary, was with him. "Where are you headed this morning?"

"I'm going to mass. What about you?"

Mary moved closer to where John stood. "That's where we're going. We can walk together." Without pausing, Mary took John by the arm and placed her gloved hand in the crook of his bent elbow.

This wasn't exactly how John had planned the morning to go. When they arrived and entered the narthex, John gazed about to see if Elizabeth was there. The cathedral's interior took his breath away with its impressive architectural elements—soaring ceilings, intricately carved details, and enormous stained glass windows in brilliant colors. The scent of beeswax candles brought John's memories back to the small chapel he'd attended in his youth.

Stuart and Mary invited John to sit with them. He still hadn't seen Elizabeth, but in this large cathedral, it was likely he might not. Because John was sitting next to Mary, and he didn't want Elizabeth to get the wrong idea, this was fine by him.

At the close of the service, John followed his friends outside. He was speaking with Mary when he saw Elizabeth out of the corner of his eye. She was getting into an open carriage with her parents, only a few feet away.

Once seated, she turned and noticed John. In that instant, Mary took John's arm in the same possessive manner she'd done earlier, and Elizabeth turned away. She gave no acknowledgement that she'd seen him. Instead, she reached into her reticule as if she was looking for something.

John wasn't sure, but it seemed as if a look of disappointment had flashed across Elizabeth's face in that brief moment their eyes had met. A short time later, the carriage pulled away, and she was gone.

CHAPTER EIGHT

E lizabeth sat at the dressing table while Sissy secured her updo with pins. The carriage would be ready to take the ladies to the market soon. It was best to arrive early and get the finest selection. The weekly routine that Elizabeth had carved out for herself felt more satisfying and full of purpose than it had when she'd first arrived in Chicago. She loved having work to do.

Monday and Thursday mornings were dedicated to shopping at the flower market. Monday afternoons, Elizabeth created the floral arrangements for the Palmer House, working from the apartment. On Tuesdays and Fridays, she worked in the studio at the store. As long as she kept Wednesdays and Saturdays open for giving or receiving at-home calls, Elizabeth's mother seemed content to let her do as she wished.

"I'll wear my pearl necklace today, Sissy," Elizabeth said. She picked up the stack of calling cards that had been left behind over the last few days and perused them.

Sissy found the necklace and put it around Elizabeth's neck. "Harold Pierce left a card behind again, miss. He came by on Saturday while you were out."

Elizabeth had been doing her best to avoid Harold Pierce, but the man was persistent. *Maybe I should give him a chance. It would make my parents happy. John's certainly not interested in me.*

Seeing John with that pretty woman on Sunday morning had been the wake-up call Elizabeth needed. She'd learned, early on, that she wasn't the only woman working at the store who'd fallen for John's charming ways.

Was he stepping out with that girl she'd seen him with? They'd seemed close—closer than just friends. Why should it have surprised her? He was entertaining, handsome, smart, and artistic. All the ladies seemed to love him. To John, she was probably nothing more than a florist who provided a service for the store.

Obviously, she'd misread him. John had a way of making everyone around him feel special. Elizabeth felt foolish for even thinking there might be something more between them. *I won't make that mistake again.*

A soft knock on the door broke the silence. Elizabeth glanced in the mirror, and behind her, she saw her mother enter the bedroom.

"We have the Wendell ball tonight, Elizabeth. Make sure you give yourself enough time to be ready this evening." Her mother walked over to the wardrobe, opened it, and began scrutinizing Elizabeth's gowns. She pulled out a robin's egg blue silk dress that Elizabeth rarely wore. "This one is lovely. Why don't you wear it later? Oh, and Elizabeth, I invited the Pierces to come here beforehand, for drinks. Harold is going to escort you tonight."

There was no point in arguing and no time either. Elizabeth needed to get to the flower market. "Yes, Mother. I'll be home in plenty of time." She considered the splint on her mother's wrist. After several weeks, it was still healing from the bike accident. A wave of sympathy and guilt washed over Elizabeth. "Would you like to come to the flower market with me today?"

Her mother smiled. "Yes—I think I would. Thank you."

***

On Tuesday, Elizabeth arrived at Marshall Field's and headed straight to the basement studio to start working. John usually had meetings in the mornings, so she would have the space all to herself—which was just how she wanted it. If she could work fast, she might avoid him altogether.

Allowing Harold Pierce to escort her to the ball the previous evening had only confirmed Elizabeth's initial feelings about the man. He was arrogant and not someone she was interested in spending more time with.

Unfortunately, her plan to give Harold another chance and forget about John had backfired. The contrasts between the two men were striking, and seeing it so clearly had only deepened the heartache she now felt.

John was confident, but not arrogant. His friendly demeanor extended to everyone he met, and he seemed genuinely interested in making those around him feel comfortable. Harold, on the other hand, never missed an opportunity to demonstrate his perceived superiority over others. Elizabeth wished she could bring herself to feel the same way about Harold that she felt about John. She wanted to make everyone happy. Why did it all have to be so complicated?

The flowers Elizabeth and her mother had picked out at the market were waiting for her in the studio. Empty vases of assorted shapes and sizes covered the table, and to her relief, it appeared the studio was empty. *I'll start with the Tearoom today.*

She chose several small vases and filled them with water. Elizabeth began pulling yellow roses from the buckets to use. The delicate fragrance reminded her of the summertime at Davenport Manor and of her friend Catherine. Had Elizabeth made the right decision in coming back to Chicago? She brought a rose close to her nose and inhaled, savoring the fresh scent—and closing her eyes, forgetting that she'd intended to hurry this morning.

The click of boots on the wood floor stirred Elizabeth out of her daydream, and she looked up to see John. Her heart felt like it skipped a beat.

"Good morning, Elizabeth. Those roses sure do smell good. I have to say, sharing a studio with a florist certainly has its perks."

"Oh, good morning, Mr. Lewis," Elizabeth said. She hoped she didn't sound too eager. "I'll try to stay out of your way. What are you working on today?"

John walked over to the corner and removed a sheet from an old stained glass window. A few sections of glass were broken, and the paint on the wood frame was chipped, but it was still remarkably beautiful. "I salvaged this from an old church that's being demolished. I'm going to sand the frame down and repaint it. It's for a bridal-themed display window."

Elizabeth gently ran her fingers across the smooth glass panes. "It's incredible."

John smiled. "Yes, this window needs some work, but something about it grabbed my attention. When the store's addition is completed, we'll have our own carpentry shop. Then we'll really get to create some wonderful props for the store. There will be a dedicated floral studio too." He paused. "Although I do like the way it is now, sharing this space with you."

Elizabeth felt her face grow warm at the compliment. "When will the construction on the addition be complete?"

"Can't say for sure—within the next three or four months, I'd imagine. I was planning on going over there today to take a peek and check on the progress. Would you like to come with me?"

Should she? "I'd like to—thank you. But I'm afraid I have too much to do here this morning."

"How about we go at lunchtime? I can wait." John flashed a bright smile.

Elizabeth's resolve weakened. How could it not? John had a way of making Elizabeth feel like her whole world lit up when he was around. She wanted to spend more time with him, even if it was at a construction site. She hoped he was unaware of the effect he had on her. "Okay. I should be able to get most of these done by then."

"Great! I'll work on this window in the meantime." John picked up a piece of sandpaper and set his attention on his project.

Noon finally arrived, and Elizabeth and John walked down the street toward the annex together. Elizabeth looked about, hoping nobody would recognize her. She didn't need anyone to report back to her mother, once again. But when she entered the new building, Elizabeth forgot about those concerns.

Inside the noisy worksite, workers were busy hammering, sawing, and moving about like industrious ants. A few curious glances were thrown Elizabeth's way, but there was work to do, so John and Elizabeth were left to look about the place on their own.

They'd entered an open atrium, surrounded by five levels of balconies. A high vaulted ceiling soared above them. In spite of its current unfinished state, Elizabeth could tell that this would eventually be a place of grandeur and elegance. She felt giddy with excitement and privileged to have an early preview.

"Have you ever been in an elevator before?" John asked.

"Yes, there are a few in Manhattan, and there's one at my father's office." She didn't tell him that she'd refused to ride in any of them.

"Well, we're finally getting elevators here too. What do you say we go up?"

Elizabeth followed John over to a long hallway that had six elevator doors. *They look so modern.* "Which one?" she laughed nervously, not wanting to admit to John that the thought of getting into a small moving cage, held only by cables, was something that frightened her..

She'd already embarrassed herself in front of John with that dramatic reaction to the fire at the market. Elizabeth didn't want him to think she was a silly girl who was afraid of everything. So, when John opened the gate for her to step into the elevator, she followed him.

The ride upstairs was uneventful and mercifully short, and though Elizabeth was well aware of their close physical proximity, she didn't mind. On the fifth floor, John led Elizabeth around the empty spaces and explained what would be going in the different areas.

"Mr. Field has big plans for that ceiling," he said, pointing up. "He's working with Mr. Tiffany to commission a glass mosaic design that will cover the entire space. I'm not sure when it will happen. Not before the store opens, but eventually."

John's enthusiasm for the store was obvious. As he gave Elizabeth the tour, it deepened her appreciation for who he was as an artist. She admired the way he could see and describe beautiful design elements in what was, at the moment, a blank canvas. He was a man of passion who loved his work—and that was extremely attractive to Elizabeth.

"Well, this was fun. Thank you for coming with me today." John looked at his watch. I should probably get back to work now."

Elizabeth and John got back on an elevator. Only this time, the elevator made a strange clunking noise before coming to a stop in between the third and fourth floors. John pushed the buttons. Nothing. They were stuck.

"Hello! Is anyone out there?" he yelled.

Elizabeth's heart started racing. "Help! Can someone please help us?"

After a few minutes of shouting, they finally heard footsteps coming closer to the elevator. "Hello? Are you stuck?" a man called down through the shaft. "Is that you, Mr. Lewis? I'll get some help! Hold tight."

Elizabeth decided to sit down on the floor while they waited. "Do you think it will be a while?"

"I'm not sure. Don't worry. They'll get us out of here." John sat down across from Elizabeth. "Are you cold? Would you like my coat?"

"I'm fine. Thank you." *What time is it? Is anyone searching for me?* There was nothing to be done but to wait. And there were indeed worse things that could happen other than being stuck in an elevator with John Lewis.

Elizabeth would take advantage of the situation and ask the question that had been on her mind the last few days. "I saw you at Holy Name on Sunday," she started, then hesitated. *How do I ask this next question without sounding too forward?*

"Yes, I'm sorry I didn't have a chance to say hello," John said, rescuing her from further awkwardness. "You were leaving when I saw you. I was there with my friends, Stuart and Mary Peterson."

"Mary Peterson...she works at the cosmetics counter, doesn't she?" Elizabeth tried to sound only casually interested.

"Yes, she's Stuart's sister. Stuart works at the store too. He was one of the first people I met when I came to Chicago."

Finally, Elizabeth boldly asked. "And Mary? Is she someone special in your life?"

John smiled. "She's a friend, that's all."

Elizabeth suddenly felt lighter—happier. But she maintained her composure, keeping her expression neutral.

"Mr. Lewis, it appears there's some kind of malfunction with the mechanical system," a voice shouted down through the elevator shaft. "The cable is stable and locked in place. You're not in danger. We have a mechanic from the elevator company on his way right now. Who's in the elevator with you?"

"Elizabeth Nordeman, sir," John answered.

Great. This isn't going to go over well when the news gets out. She braced herself for another run-in with her mother for going somewhere, unchaperoned, with John Lewis. But she also hoped the mechanic would take his time getting there. As long as they weren't in danger, Elizabeth was quite happy with the current situation.

It was getting cold. Elizabeth shivered and rubbed her arms to stay warm. Without asking again, John took off his suit jacket and moved closer to Elizabeth, putting it around her shoulders.

"So, you asked about Mary, and now I have a question for you. Is there a special man in your life?" John asked.

"No, there isn't." Elizabeth watched John's face as she said the words. Her heart skipped a beat when John's mouth curved into a slight smile.

Sitting on the floor of the elevator, side by side, Elizabeth and John's conversation soon moved from those first awkward questions to something more comfortable. John was easy to talk to, and Elizabeth didn't even notice how much time was going by. She told him about her childhood in New York, her brother, Samuel, and her best friend, Catherine. John entertained Elizabeth with stories about his siblings and life on his farm growing up. His family sounded like people she'd love to meet.

It wasn't without a little disappointment when Elizabeth heard the voice from the elevator shaft calling out to them, telling them it was all over. They'd fixed the problem.

"Push the button to take you down now, Mr. Lewis. It should work." It did.

When Elizabeth exited the elevator with John on the first floor, there were dozens of construction workers waiting for them, clapping and cheering for the successful rescue. They'd been stuck for nearly two hours, but it had only felt like a few wonderful minutes.

John shook hands with several men, thanking them, and he good-naturedly laughed at the teasing comments he received. Elizabeth smiled shyly, said a quick thank you to the workers, and ducked her head as she made her way to the entrance. She didn't want word of this getting out, but it was too late. A man with a camera took her picture, and another man with a notebook and pen was shouting questions. Ignoring them, Elizabeth hurried out to the street and walked toward the Palmer House.

CHAPTER NINE

A telegram was on John's desk when he returned to his office..

I'll be in Chicago October 10th.
Horace

John glanced at the calendar on the wall. That was today, and it was three in the afternoon already. Would his older brother be waiting for him at his apartment when he got there? John was curious for the reason behind this rare visit, but happy, nevertheless.

The brothers were stark opposites in personality and interests, even though they could pass as twins by appearance. John and Horace had always been close, but the two had rarely seen one another over the last five years. They'd both been working hard. It would be nice to see his brother.

Outside the window, dark clouds were rolling in off Lake Michigan. It looked like a storm was brewing. *Going home earlier than usual might be a good idea.*

Ordinarily, John might have been in a bad mood after losing a couple of hours of work from being trapped in an elevator. But nothing could dampen his spirits now—not the rain clouds and not the thought of the hours he'd need to make up for the lost time. How could he complain when he'd just spent that time with Elizabeth? Blissful. That's what it had been. Had he sensed correctly that perhaps his feelings for the beautiful florist might actually be reciprocated? Was it too good to be true?

John was whistling to himself as he turned on the lamp at his desk and sat down. He tried to concentrate for the next few minutes as he sorted through his mail, but it was no use. He was drawn back to Elizabeth and their time in the construction site elevator again and again. The way pink crept across her cheeks when he explained Mary was just a friend, the way her face softened when she talked about her family. It was time to call it a day. John put on his coat. When he did, he caught the faintest whiff of Elizabeth's perfume she'd been wearing earlier.

Outside, the skies opened, sending a downpour upon the poor souls who were unfortunate enough to be out on the streets. Hopefully, Elizabeth had already made it home safely. She'd disappeared rather quickly when the reporter appeared. He understood. The press liked to play up any story that even hinted at impropriety with society girls like Elizabeth. Though it had all been innocent, he could see how, a young, unmarried woman, being trapped in an elevator with him, might appear scandalous. He prayed the reporter would have the decency to keep Elizabeth's name out of the story.

John finally reached his apartment, sorely regretting not bringing an umbrella. He was thoroughly soaked through to the skin, and cold, but his misery was quickly forgotten when he opened his front door to find his brother, Horace, standing at the stove making beef stew.

"Horace! Good to see you, brother. I was hoping I'd left the apartment unlocked today. I'm glad you let yourself in. I just got your telegram." John took off his hat. "What brings you to the city?"

"Hey, John." Horace took the pot off the burner and turned to give his brother a strong slap on the back. "I had to come see if you were still alive. I haven't seen you forever! Glad you didn't move. That would have been awkward if I'd been in the wrong apartment."

John hung up his wet coat and hat, then moved behind the folding screen separating the living from the sleeping area as he changed into dry clothes. "How are Mother and Father?"

"They both send their love, and Mother sent that tin of cookies over on the table. Father is using a cane to get around now, but he's still strong enough to mind the animals." Horace set two bowls of beef stew on the table. "It's the only meal I know how to make, sorry about that."

"Hey, I like beef stew—no complaints here. Thank you." John took a bite of hot potato. How long can you stay?"

"The crops didn't do so well this year. I was hoping to supplement the income for the farm with some work here over the winter. Alice and her children are staying with Mom and Dad while I'm here." Alice was their older sister, a widow with two teenage boys, Elijah and Don, and a seven-year-old daughter, Ida.

"You're always welcome here. Want me to check at the store? I can see if there are any openings."

"I'd appreciate that." Horace took a bite of his sandwich. "I don't want to be a burden. I'll contribute, and I can sleep on the davenport." He paused. "So, tell me, what's going on with you?"

The brothers had already finished their sandwiches, but John was still hungry. Seeing that the rain had stopped, he suggested they continue with another dinner course at the pub downstairs. After settling in at the bar, John told Horace about Elizabeth.

"It's about time, brother," Horace said with a jab to John's arm.

"I don't know." John sighed. "Her last name is Nordeman—as in Nordeman Insurance. I'm afraid I can't offer her the luxurious life she's accustomed to."

Horace took a sip of beer. "Give yourself more credit than that. Though I'm the last person you'd want to take relationship advice from." Horace, at thirty, was still a bachelor. He'd been engaged once, but his fiancé had called off the wedding at the last moment, leaving him heartbroken. "Maybe you can introduce me to some pretty shop girls while I'm around," he said, laughing.

Stuart Peterson wandered into the pub, and John waved him over, introducing him to his brother. Seeing Stuart gave him an idea. Stuart's sister, Mary, might like to meet Horace. John would make that happen.

At the end of the evening, as the men were leaving, Stuart said, "Horace, the store needs another driver. If you're interested, come by to-morrow morning—first thing. We'll get you set up."

***

It was still early morning when John stopped by the tearoom to talk with Mr. Walters, the maître d and found Elizabeth there, delivering her floral arrangements.

Mr. Walters had been pleased with the addition of Miss Nordeman to the team, and he'd ceased his endless complaints about the center-pieces, at long last. But today, the grumpy man had something else to complain about. Mr. Walters didn't like the new rugs John had purchased for the restaurant, so he was there to confer with the man and see what could be done about it.

The empty tearoom wouldn't be open for yet another hour, so the two men sat down together in the back. Elizabeth quietly replaced the old centerpiece at their table, then nodded a greeting to Mr. Walters and John before moving on.

John forgot about everything else for a moment and watched Elizabeth as she continued with her work. Not being a person to hide his feelings well, John tried to appear nonchalant. It wasn't until he noticed the maître d watching him, with a smirk of smug satisfaction, that the realization sunk in—he'd been caught. John would have to be more careful with how he interacted with Elizabeth when in front of the other employees. Gossip spread through this place quickly.

Later on, back downstairs in the studio, when nobody else was around, John and Elizabeth began a friendly conversation about the upcoming World's Fair and whether or not George Washington Ferris's wheel idea would actually work.

"It's impossible," John said. "The thing won't be able to revolve, though I do admire the man. He has vision and real courage for even trying."

"I think it will work, and I intend to be one of the first people to ride it," Elizabeth said as she placed the finishing touches on a large arrangement of fragrant yellow roses that would go to the millinery department.

"If it does, I'll go with you." The last time John had been near the fairgrounds, the great wheel that everyone had been talking about was nothing more than a big hole in the ground. Supposedly, it would rival the Eiffel Tower in height when it was finished—*if* it was ever finished. Right now, rumor was the fair committee had eliminated funding for the project.

"You know what could work for a window display?" Elizabeth seemed thoughtful. "You could do something like a miniature of what the Ferris's wheel is supposed to look like and combine it with some women's ready-to-wear ensembles. The *Tribune* published some drawings the other day that you could use for inspiration."

"I like that idea." Elizabeth's suggestion sounded whimsical and fun. "Would you be interested in working on it together?"

"Oh, yes. I would love that!"

"I'll work on some sketches and see what I can come up with." John looked at the floral arrangement Elizabeth had just completed. "That must be heavy. Why don't I carry that vase up to millinery for you? You could come with me, and after we drop it off, we could take a peek around and start getting an idea of what merchandise might work for the display."

A few minutes later, John and Elizabeth were looking at silk scarves when John sensed someone watching them. He turned, but nobody was there. Moving downstairs to see the shoes, John continued to feel as if they were being followed.

"This is so fun. Thank you for letting me help you. I've always wanted to learn how you put the window displays together." Elizabeth didn't seem to notice anything out of the ordinary.

"I could use the help, and you've got a good eye. I'm glad we can work together on this." John smiled. "I think we've got enough to get started. We can talk more next week. We've got plenty of time."

"Well, if we're done here, I think I'll go back down to the studio to get my coat and hat. Then I'll be going." Elizabeth smiled sweetly and waved. "Bye, John."

John said goodbye, then started straightening the shoes on the shelf, which he'd noticed were in a state of disarray. He felt a firm hand grip his elbow from behind. Startled, he turned, nearly knocking the person in the face. A skinny weasel-faced man was glaring at him, with what was probably intended to be a look of intimidation—Harold Pierce. "Were you following me?" John asked, more irritated than intimidated.

"What were you doing with Miss Nordeman?" Harold asked, ignoring John's question. "You seem awfully familiar with her."

Mr. Field had warned John to keep Elizabeth's work at the store discreet. She was to be considered a private contractor, not an employee—but something about Harold's demeanor told John to keep even that to himself. "Excuse me? She's a customer. I was helping her."

"She's *my* girl. That's who she is—and I didn't like what I saw just now. Stay away from her, or I'll make sure you lose your job." He squeezed John's elbow tighter for emphasis before letting go. Harold didn't give John an opportunity to respond before he walked away. But before he left the shoe department, he knocked several pairs of shoes to the floor.

"What was that all about?" Everett, the manager of the shoe department, had watched the whole exchange. "Wasn't that Harold Pierce?"

"Yes, it was. I don't know what his problem is. He's crazy. John knew better than to let someone like Harold get to him, but the exchange had rattled him more than he cared to admit. It was just another unwelcome reminder that he was fooling himself if he thought he had any kind of chance with Elizabeth Nordeman.

CHAPTER TEN

Elizabeth and her mother were having tea together in the sitting room of their apartment when the topic of Harold Pierce came up.

"Darling, it seems to me that you've been avoiding Harold Pierce. You were gone again yesterday when he came to call, and you've been spending a lot more time at the store recently." Her mother lifted her teacup, but her focus remained fixed on Elizabeth. "Tell me what's going on."

Elizabeth placed a sugar cube in her tea and stirred it slowly. How should she answer Mother? She didn't want to be disrespectful, but she did want to be honest—and her fear was that her true feelings about Harold Pierce were not what her mother wanted to hear.

Elizabeth really wanted to tell her mother about John Lewis. But was it too soon? They were nothing more than friends. Elizabeth wasn't sure if John felt the same way about her that she felt about him. And her mother would probably have a problem with John's background. He wasn't rich.

"Mother, I don't want Harold Pierce to be calling on me anymore. I don't feel any differently about him now than I did in the beginning. I feel worse! He's insufferable, and I don't enjoy his company."

Her mother sighed, but she was a reasonable woman, and she loved Elizabeth. "You're twenty-one years old, and many of your friends have already married. I just want you to be happy." She took a macaroon from the tiered stand and put it on her plate. "I think you need to tell Harold how you feel the next time you see him. I'll support you. Perhaps Chicago isn't the right place for you to meet a husband. Maybe we should have stayed in New York."

"Thank you, but I'm happy here, Mother. I know it didn't seem that way at first, but I love my work at the store. You don't need to worry about me. I'm not an old maid—yet. I have plenty of time." She put down her tea. "Did I tell you that Mr. Lewis is letting me help him with the window displays?" Elizabeth bit off a piece of her scone and tried to appear casual. But she was watching her mother's expression closely to see how she reacted to that last bit of information.

Her mother frowned but remained silent.

Annette gently knocked on the door before coming into the room . "Mrs. Nordeman, Mrs. Palmer is here to see you. Should I show her in?"

"Yes, thank you, Annette."

Their housekeeper left, and her mother gave Elizabeth a piercing glance. "We'll finish this conversation later." Then, seeing Mrs. Palmer already in the doorway, she stood, and smiled broadly. "Bertha! How lovely to see you. Come, please take a seat."

Once again, rescued by Mrs. Palmer. This woman is something like a fairy godmother. "Mrs. Palmer, how do you do?"

"I'm very well. Thank you. I've been very pleased with the flower arrangements you've been creating for the lobby," Mrs. Palmer said. Taking a sip of the tea Annette had just poured for her, she paused. "As you ladies know, I'm serving as President of the Board of Lady Managers for the fair. In that capacity, I'll be traveling to Washington D.C. next week." She set down her cup. "I'm going to speak to congress about my request for a coin to commemorate the fair. Another friend who was going to come with me has sadly taken ill, and she won't be able to travel. I came to see if you, Patricia, might be interested in accompanying me. We'll have a private rail car, of course, and it's only for a few days. What do you say?"

Elizabeth's mother seemed genuinely touched. "How kind of you to think of me for such an honor, Bertha. I need to discuss it with Cornelius first. May I send you my answer tomorrow?" It was merely a formality. It was obvious that she had already decided to go.

"Of course," Mrs. Palmer said. "I don't like to travel alone, and Potter simply can't get away at a time like this."

With her mother traveling, Elizabeth would have some extra time to figure out what was actually happening between herself and John—and whether or not there was anything she needed to tell her parents. Also, the additional hours Elizabeth was planning to spend at the store, helping with the new window display, would now go unnoticed. Yes, Mrs. Palmer's invitation couldn't have come at a better time.

***

A few days later, Elizabeth went to Union Station with her mother and Mrs. Palmer to see them off. They rode along the city streets in the Palmer's carriage. On the seat was a *Chicago Tribune* from that morning.

Her mother glanced at the headlines, then reacted in a mix of horror and surprise at something she saw. "Elizabeth, your picture is on the front page!" She took a moment to read. "You were trapped in an elevator? Why didn't you say anything? And what were you doing there, anyway?" She held to the belief that a well-bred woman never appeared in the papers, and the only exceptions were when they married and when they died.

Elizabeth had forgotten about the reporter with the camera. Her face grew hot with embarrassment. "I didn't know they got a picture. I'm sorry. It was hardly worth mentioning. I was just taking a tour of the new part of Marshall Field's with Mr. Lewis when the elevator got stuck. We weren't in any danger. I promise. That's why I never said anything. I didn't want to concern you with it."

Elizabeth could tell from her mother's rigid posture that she was more upset than she was letting on. Once again, she had Mrs. Palmer to thank. The woman had no idea her presence was keeping a lid on what would otherwise have been a contentious situation between mother and daughter.

Her mother took a deep breath. "It says here, Mr. Lewis was stuck on the elevator too. Do you know how that looks? It's *entirely* inappropriate. Who is this Mr. Lewis, anyway?"

This was not the way Elizabeth wanted to tell her mother about John.

"You met him at the store, Mother. He's a gentleman. He kept me calm the whole time we were stuck on the elevator by telling me funny stories."

"I don't like this," her mother said, but she left the conversation unfinished because the carriage had arrived at the station.

"It will all blow over soon," Mrs. Palmer said, patting Elizabeth's hand. But it wasn't the public's perception of the article that had Elizabeth concerned. It was her mother's. Nevertheless, Elizabeth smiled gratefully and nodded.

The women said their goodbyes, and Elizabeth stood and waved as the train pulled out of the station.

***

Elizabeth didn't like upsetting her parents. Even her father, who usually came to her defense, had gruffly reprimanded her at dinner that evening. He, too, had read the story about the elevator incident in the newspaper. He wasn't pleased that his daughter had put herself in a position where her reputation could be compromised.

Later on, when Elizabeth and her father were both quietly reading in the library, she asked about Ferris's wheel and how far along it was. For several months, all work on the wheel had ceased, and it seemed as if George Ferris's project wasn't going to happen—but it was finally moving along now.

She wanted to tell her father about the window display she'd been invited to work on, but Elizabeth also wanted to gently drop John's name into the conversation in a complementary way. It wouldn't be good for her father to be left with a negative impression of John, which was the only one he seemed to have at the moment.

Then, she had a better idea. She would arrange a meeting between the men. She was sure, once her father met John, that he would like him.

"Mr. Lewis is a talented artist, Father, and I appreciate how he's given me so many opportunities at the store with the flowers and now the window displays. We're working on a display that will feature a model of Ferris's wheel." Elizabeth put down her book. "I have a favor to ask of you. I know the fairgrounds aren't open to the public yet, but do you think it would be possible for Mr. Lewis, you, and me, to visit the site of the Great Wheel and speak with Mr. Ferris? I would like to repay Mr. Lewis for his kindness, and I think it would mean a great deal to him."

Her father considered Elizabeth's request for a moment. "I'll see what I can do." But the man was perceptive, and he knew his daughter well. He had more questions. "Tell me more about this, Mr. Lewis. Do you spend a lot of time with him?"

"We share a work studio, and he's very kind..." Elizabeth stopped speaking when she noticed her father no longer seemed to hear what she was saying. His face had gone white, and he was clutching his shoulder as if in pain. Her father dropped his glass, spilling red wine on the expensive rug. "Father! What's wrong?"

The housekeeper, Annette, hearing the commotion, rushed into the room. Elizabeth, feeling breathless with fright, told her to call for a doctor.

"Don't worry, Elizabeth," her father said between labored breaths. "It's just a little chest pain. I'll be okay."

But when the doctor arrived, he was concerned, even after her father said he was feeling better, and he ordered Father to rest for the next few days.

Elizabeth tried without success to relax. She'd already lost her brother, and now she was afraid she was going to lose her father as well. The next day, she sent a telegram to her mother, letting her know the barest details of what happened, with assurances that Father was okay now. She didn't want her mother to panic, especially when she was so far away.

Elizabeth had no intention of leaving her father's side until the doctor indicated it would be okay for him to get out of bed. Through Sissy, she sent another message to John, letting him know she would not be able to come into the store that week. Elizabeth understood her father, a man who never stopped working, would have a difficult time resting, so she sat near his bed and read out loud to him whenever he was awake.

Several days later, having finished reading the Sherlock Holmes stories her father loved, Elizabeth searched for another book on the shelves in the library. She took one called, *Catena Aurea*, that she had seen her father reading many times and brought it back to his room. Her father was nearly asleep already, but Elizabeth settled back into her chair by his bed and opened the book to the place where a bookmark had been placed.

"'It is not that we keep His commandments first and that then He loves but that He loves us and then we keep His commandments. This is that grace which is revealed to the humble but hidden from the proud.'" The passage was a quote, attributed to Augustine of Hippo.

Elizabeth looked over at her father, who was now sleeping soundly. He seemed older, and he was still weak from his incident a couple of nights ago. She hadn't prayed in a long time and didn't feel deserving of such a privilege. Her dear brother would still be with them today if it weren't for her disobedience.

She'd never be able to forgive herself, and she'd often shuddered in shame at the thought of what God must feel about her. But as she thought about the words of Augustine, she decided she would try praying tonight, on behalf of her father. *Maybe God will listen, even if I don't deserve it.*

CHAPTER ELEVEN

John would have to tell his brother to go home without him. Again. It would be another late night at work. With Elizabeth still gone, he'd need to make the flower arrangements for the store by himself, on top of his other responsibilities. Her absence highlighted the degree to which John had come to depend on her in the few short months since she'd first walked into the store asking for a job.

In the time that his brother had been in town, they'd managed to have dinner together just once. Still, in spite of only seeing Horace during brief moments in passing, and on the walk to work each morning, it felt good to have him around.

The stables at the back of the store were quiet when John wandered in, looking for his brother. A few contented nickers and neighs greeted him as he walked past the stalls. Most of the drivers and grooms had already left for the evening. Even the horses were resting after their day of work pulling the delivery wagons. Still, John couldn't rest until he'd seen to every detail throughout the store, ensuring it was at its best when it opened tomorrow morning. Marshall Field, who'd been in New York the past couple of weeks, would be back—and everything had to be perfect.

Horace was brushing one of the Cleveland Bays when John found him. "Hey, Brother. I think it's going to be another late night. Don't bother waiting for me."

"You need dinner. Why don't I go to the pub, get us some fish and chips, and bring them back to the store? Will you be in the studio?"

John was hungry and thankful for the offer of both food and company. "Thank you—yes. I'm sorry I haven't been around much. How's it going down here? Do you enjoy the work?"

"I do—and no apology necessary. I'll catch you up when I get back. I'm hungry too." Horace put away the brush and slipped on his coat as he prepared to go.

An hour later, John was in his studio, snipping greenery and arranging a vase of roses for the concierge desk when Horace reappeared with dinner. It smelled delicious. John didn't realize how hungry he was until his belly growled when Horace opened the bag. John cleared a spot on the table, and the men quickly devoured the food.

Horace filled John in on everything that had been happening over the past week with his work as a delivery driver. John was happy that his brother had been warmly welcomed into the community of employees who worked at the store. His guilt over working late every night was eased somewhat when he learned that Horace had been invited the last three nights to go out for a beer with Stuart Peterson and his friends.

When Horace mentioned that he'd met Mary Peterson and that he'd like to get to know her better, he seemed hesitant, as if he was unsure if his brother would approve. John assured him that not only did he approve, but he was happy to hear it.

Horace wiped some salt from the chips off his mouth with a napkin and grinned. "How are things going with Miss Nordeman?"

John told Horace about the message he'd received that day when Elizabeth's maid, Sissy, came to the store, telling him her father was ill. "We were working on a design together for a new window display. She has great ideas. She suggested a World's Fair theme, featuring a model of Ferris's wheel. I'm not sure if I should wait for her to return, or if I should move ahead without her. I don't know how long she'll be gone or how serious her father's illness is."

"I can help you. You want me to build the wheel? I'm pretty good with a hammer and saw," Horace said.

John was grateful for the help, and he was impressed when his brother, using nothing more than the sketches John had drawn, created a realistic model of the proposed Great Wheel.

Over the next few evenings, after the store closed, the brothers worked together into the early morning hours. Though John had been looking forward to working with Elizabeth on the project, he was enjoying the extra time with Horace, and this project required the skills of a carpenter more than a florist. He'd have to find another project to collaborate on with Elizabeth.

***

A week later, when all the pieces were ready to be placed in the window, Elizabeth still hadn't returned to work, so John went ahead and installed everything without her. On the morning of the reveal, he was both excited and proud, yet also a bit wistful, thinking about how much fun this project would have been with Elizabeth. It was his best work to date, full of whimsy and eye-catching details that showcased the store's products beautifully.

Standing outside on the sidewalk, studying his creation, John smiled when he saw a little boy point at the window and exclaim, "Mama, I want to go in there!" It was unfortunate that he couldn't give Elizabeth any of the credit for her idea, but Mr. Field had warned John to keep her involvement at the store discreet. So, he stayed quiet.

The Great Wheel themed window was a success. Mr. Field was pleased and had sent a message to John's office, issuing a rare compliment, along with an invitation to join him for lunch at the Union League Club that day.

John was planning to make a special request when he met with his boss. He'd wanted to order some wax mannequins for the store for some time now, and with the current level of attention the store was receiving for its window displays, it seemed like a good time to ask. The mannequins were expensive, but the best stores in Paris and New York were using them, and John thought it was high time Marshall Field's did too.

So, it was with some confusion and surprise that later on, seated in the sumptuous dining room at the club, John's request was met with loud laughter—followed by a firm no.

Mr. Field wiped his eyes and composed himself. "Sorry, John, I must explain myself." He stifled another laugh. "When I was in New York last week, I walked by a department store. I was looking at the window displays when I nearly jumped out of my boots in horror. The wax mannequin in the window had melted, causing its head to fall off and rest on its chest! Once I got over my initial scare, I thought it was the funniest thing ever and so did a lot of other people. I will never forget that sight. But neither will I allow my store to become the laughingstock of the city with melting mannequins in the windows. The answer is no—but what else can I help you with, son?"

A waiter approached the table to take their order. "Steak, medium rare, and a baked potato, please," John said. *I could get used to this.*

After the waiter left, John grinned. The thought of Mr. Field coming upon the mannequin with the misplaced head in New York was funny. He couldn't blame the man. It was understandable why Mr. Field wanted nothing to do with wax mannequins after seeing that.

John took a sip of coffee and considered Mr. Field's question. Something more serious was on John's mind. "I do have a question about Miss Nordeman, our florist. She's been absent this past week because her father has been ill. I know you're acquainted with her family, so I was wondering if you might know how Mr. Nordeman is faring? I've been concerned, and I've wanted to inquire personally, but I've been uncertain over the propriety of my doing so."

Mr. Field leaned back in his chair and studied John. Then he pulled a white rose from the centerpiece on the table, snapping off the stem and placing it in a buttonhole on his lapel. "Perhaps it would be good for the florist to receive flowers for a change. It would only be right. Put together an arrangement for Miss Nordeman and her family. Say it's from the store, and let them know we're thinking of them, then have it sent it to the Palmer House. I'm on several committees with Mr. Nordeman, and from what I heard, he's expected to make a recovery." John's boss paused. "You care about Miss Nordeman? In a personal way?" He sighed. "I warned you, didn't I?"

"Yes, you did, sir."

Mr. Field frowned, and John nervously waited for what was coming next. "I'll see if I can arrange an introduction between Mr. Nordeman and yourself when he's feeling better. If you want to get to know Miss Nordeman better, you'll have to go through her father. He won't be easy to impress, and her mother will be even more difficult."

"Yes, sir. Thank you." John was surprised and considered Mr. Field's offer the greatest of kindnesses. His boss was going out on a limb by inviting him into his private club and various high society events. Formal introductions, like this, were not to be taken lightly. It showed a high level of trust.

John wasn't sure how to respond. But the grin he couldn't hide probably said it all.

CHAPTER TWELVE

Chicago's first snow of the year had arrived. Delicate crystalline flakes swirled about in the wind. Elizabeth pulled her scarf up around her face to protect it from the stinging cold. She was walking down State Street with Sissy, along her well-worn route from the Palmer House to Marshall Field's. The snow beneath her feet was still only a light dusting. The whole city appeared as if it was covered in powdered sugar. It felt good to be outside again, no matter the weather, and she was excited to get back to work.

The past couple of weeks had been trying and frightening. Elizabeth's mother had returned from Washington the day before, anxious to see her husband, and relieved to find him in relatively good health. It was hard for Elizabeth to see her usually strong and vibrant father laid up in bed, though she was sure it had been even more difficult for him. But today, he went back to his office, ignoring the protests of his wife. Once the doctor had given him a report of improved health, her father wouldn't hear of taking one more day of rest.

"I won't be around forever," her father had said. "Elizabeth, I want to make sure you're taken care of. It's time you settled down."

Elizabeth thought about his words. She wanted to give her father some peace. The family business was intended to pass to Samuel, her brother. But now, it was her duty to find a suitable husband. She owed it to her family. Her future marriage would have to be a business arrangement if nothing else, even if this meant putting her personal feelings aside.

Approaching the store, Elizabeth gazed at the window display on the corner. There it was —Ferris's Great Wheel—or at least a six-foot replica of it. It was wonderful. But it was her idea. She would have liked to have been involved.

Sissy's eyes grew wide with wonder. "It's spectacular! I can't wait to see the real one when it's completed."

Elizabeth didn't want to hear it. She felt cheated and a little angry, though it was impossible not to acknowledge that John had good reason to do the window without her. *Of course, he'd move forward with our plans for the window. It wasn't John's fault that I've been gone.* She took a deep breath, attempting to calm her emotions.

Elizabeth said goodbye to Sissy, who promised to return in a few hours for the walk home, and then Elizabeth continued into the store. As she made her way downstairs to the basement, Elizabeth hoped John wouldn't be in the studio. She was annoyed with him, but more so, with herself. She shouldn't have put so much hope into creating the window display together. Elizabeth believed she'd been, *out of sight, and out of mind*, as far as John was concerned.

The store had sent a beautiful bouquet to the apartment with a card, wishing her father well. It was a nice gesture—but Elizabeth hadn't heard from John. Nothing. The whole time she'd been gone. She'd thought, at the very least, their friendship would have warranted a card.

I'll no longer make a fool of myself. As far as John Lewis is concerned, I'll be keeping things strictly professional. Also, from now on, I'll be keeping my ideas to myself.

As she slipped out the door a few hours later, a wash of relief flooded over Elizabeth. She had completed her day without a trace of Mr. John Lewis in sight.

***

"Are you going to the flower market this morning?" Elizabeth's father lowered his newspaper to look at his daughter as she sat down across from him in the breakfast room.

"Yes, I am." Elizabeth took a piece of hot toast and spread butter over it, watching it melt.

"I'm taking the carriage to that part of the city in a few minutes. You and Sissy can catch a ride with me." He went back to reading his paper.

"Thank you."

Annette walked in, smiled, and poured coffee into Elizabeth's cup. The rich nutty aroma wafted up with the steam.

"Do you and Mr. Lewis still want to meet with Mr. Ferris? I could set something up this week."

Elizabeth had forgotten about her request. The reminder stung. Over the past couple of weeks, since returning to work, she'd tried to avoid John. He'd been friendly, as always, and probably wasn't even aware of how his actions had hurt her. *There's no need to introduce Father to John now.* "Oh— thank you, but it's not necessary. I don't think I'll have time this week."

Her father nodded and took a sip of coffee. "By the way, Marshall Field introduced me to John Lewis yesterday. We had lunch together at the club. He's a nice fellow. He told me you helped with the design for the front corner window, the one with the model of Ferris's Great Wheel. It seems he's quite impressed with your work." He set down his coffee cup and smiled. "I'm proud of you."

Elizabeth tried to hide her surprise by taking a bite of toast. She nearly choked on it. *Maybe I was a little harsh in my judgment of John. I might have jumped to conclusions about his motives.* But she kept those thoughts to herself. "Thank you. I didn't really do anything except make a suggestion. I can't take any credit. It was already done when I went back to work the other day."

"Well, if you change your mind about wanting to meet George Ferris—just let me know. There isn't much to see yet, but it will be quite something when it all comes together."

It was time to change the subject. Elizabeth didn't want to think about John—or Ferris's Wheel. "Yes, thank you. I will, but I have something else to tell you. My friend, Catherine, and her husband, Harry, are going to be in Chicago for a few days. Harry had some business to take care of here in Chicago, and Catherine is coming too, so we can see each other. They're going to be staying right here at the Palmer House."

"Oh? That's wonderful, dear. I'm happy to hear it. When do they arrive?"

"In two days."

"Aha, well, I wish I could see them, but I won't be here. In two days, I'm returning to New York. I need to take care of some business, and I won't be back for at least several days."

Elizabeth frowned. "I thought you had someone else taking care of business right now. You nearly *died* a few weeks ago. Is it really a good idea to travel?"

"I wasn't going to die. You're a bit overdramatic, dear. I'll be fine. Mr. Bancroft has given his notice. I need to find his replacement. I'll be happy when I can hand the reins of the business over for good—God willing, to your husband, whoever that will be. I'm getting too old for this."

Elizabeth felt a familiar sense of guilt creeping through her thoughts, like a pernicious vine that refused to die. Her father should be enjoying his retirement right now. Samuel was supposed to be running the company. "May I go with you to New York? I could learn how to run our business."

"And have you miss your friend Catherine's visit? I won't hear of it," her father said.

Elizabeth wasn't surprised by his response, but she was disappointed. Her brother hadn't even wanted to go to business school, and he'd never wanted to take over the company—but as the only son of Cornelius Nordeman, and a dutiful one at that, he'd gone along with his father's plans.

On the other hand, Elizabeth had always loved studying Samuel's textbooks, and she'd often helped him write his papers. She'd always been the one who really wanted to run the company. But what could be done? Women ran households and nurtured children—they did not run companies. Her father refused to consider the idea. A small floral business, really, nothing more than a glorified *hobby*, was one thing, but running the family's insurance company was out of the question as far as he was concerned.

Missing out on Catherine's visit would have been terrible. Elizabeth could concede that point. But taking another absence from her work as a florist would have been preferable to continuing with the awkward encounters she faced every time she saw John Lewis—even if it meant he'd probably find someone else to take her place. Her feelings for that man were more mixed-up and confused than they'd ever been. Every time she thought of him, her head hurt. It would be easier just to avoid him.

"Well, Father, if you don't want me to go with you, please consider taking Mother. I don't want you to be alone if you fall ill again."

"I'll ask her." Her father smiled. "You're always looking out for me, and I don't know what I'd do without you. But please don't worry. I'll be fine."

***

"Let's go shopping today," Catherine said. "I want to see where you've been working."

Elizabeth looked up from the needlepoint she'd been working on. The two friends were in the sitting room of the Nordeman's apartment. Catherine's presence over the past couple of days had been a welcome distraction from Elizabeth's current troubles. "That sounds like fun. But don't let my mother hear you say that I work," she said with a wink. "We've come to a compromise. As long as I refer to floristry as my hobby, she's more accepting of what I'm doing." Elizabeth put down her work and peered out the window. There wasn't much to see. The view from the top floor was obscured by a mixture of thick, sooty smoke and a gray, cloudy mist. "Do you want to walk to the store?"

"Yes," Catherine said, "I'll just need to stop by my room downstairs and get my cloak."

It had recently snowed, and the streets were a frozen mess. Once they were outside, Catherine and Elizabeth held onto each other's arms, stepping gingerly to avoid slipping on the icy sidewalks. She'd been foolish for suggesting they walk outside in these conditions. Though Catherine was still as slim as ever, she'd confided to her that she was expecting a baby in the spring. Her friend was glowing with excitement when she'd told Elizabeth.

When they finally reached the front door of Marshall Field's, both women felt like they'd been on a walk through the arctic. They headed straight to the tearoom so they could get something warm to drink. "Good morning, ladies. Would you like a table by the window?" Walter asked.

"Miss Nordeman—hello! You and your friend are welcome to sit at my table," Bertha Palmer said, sitting nearby. She looked like a queen, adorned in her fabulous jewels, even at this early hour of the day.

"Ah, Mrs. Palmer! Good morning and thank you. This is my dear friend, Catherine Davenport, from New York. Catherine, may I introduce you to Mrs. Palmer." Pleasantries were exchanged as the women sat down together.

Walter took the women's coats and hats and called a waiter over to the table. "Hot chocolate for me, please," Elizabeth said.

Mrs. Palmer pointed toward the pink and white rose centerpiece in the middle of the table. "This is your design—is it not? It's beautiful."

"It is, and thank you, ma'am," Elizabeth said, trying to sound humble. Was it wrong to feel some pride at hearing Mrs. Palmer's compliment?

After a few minutes of conversation, John Lewis walked into the tearoom. He smiled at Elizabeth and nodded a greeting. She smiled shyly in return. He walked over to the maître d' stand to speak with Walter. The sight of John sent her heart racing. She picked up her teacup and pretended to study the floral pattern. Elizabeth took a deep breath, hoping the color creeping into her cheeks wouldn't betray her feelings.

Catherine noticed everything. "Who is that?" she asked.

"Oh, that's Mr. Lewis."

"Mr. Lewis?" Catherine grinned. Elizabeth wanted to kick her under the table.

"Is he the man who does the beautiful window displays?" Mrs. Palmer asked, turning her head in John's direction. "I'd like to meet him."

How could she refuse Mrs. Palmer? Fortunately, the coldness Elizabeth had felt toward him over the past few weeks had begun to thaw. She caught John's eye and gave a little wave, indicating he was welcome to come over and say hello.

"Miss Nordeman, ladies, good morning," John said, as he approached their table.

Elizabeth made the introductions, and Mrs. Palmer invited John to sit down. He was a man who seemed at ease with anyone, even the venerable Mrs. Palmer—a quality that was endearing to Elizabeth.

Mrs. Palmer motioned for a nearby waiter to bring John some coffee. "I know you're probably busy with work right now, Mr. Lewis, but please, stay awhile and have a visit with us." She paused, and then, her face lit up as if she'd just had an idea. "Elizabeth, your parents are still in New York. correct?"

"Yes, ma'am."

"Well, I don't want you to be alone, so if you don't already have a prior engagement, please let me host you and your friends for dinner tonight at my home. It's terribly last minute, I know, and I don't mean to put you on the spot—but it would be my pleasure. This includes you, too, Mr. Lewis." Mrs. Palmer had a twinkle in her eye.

Is she playing matchmaker again? "Thank you, Mrs. Palmer. Your invitation is very kind," Elizabeth said. *How can I say no?*

Catherine, who seemed to be in on Mrs. Palmer's scheme, gave a broad smile. "We would be delighted to come. Thank you!"

"Lovely. And will Mr. Davenport be joining us as well?"

"Yes, ma'am, I'm sure he'll be delighted," Catherine said.

"And you, Mr. Lewis?" Mrs. Palmer gave him a look that indicated it wasn't really a question but a summons.

"It would be an honor, ma'am. Thank you," John said.

That was how Elizabeth found herself seated next to John in the glittering dining room at the Palmer mansion later that evening. It had all happened faster than she could have anticipated. She'd been outmaneuvered by Mrs. Palmer and Catherine.

Did John realize what kind of game those two were playing? And if he did, did he mind? Elizabeth still wasn't sure if his attention was toward her, and if the way he made her feel special was merely the way he behaved toward all women—or if the spark she felt when they were together was real.

CHAPTER THIRTEEN

The Palmer's mansion on Lake Shore Drive was impressive. Some people called it a castle, and John could see why. With its stone and turrets, it harkened to medieval days. The newspapers said it was the largest private residence in Chicago.

The wildly varying architectural styles, the knobless doors requiring admission by a servant, and the rumored fortune spent on its construction all created a mysterious allure and curiosity among the people of Chicago. But they could only speculate about the inside appearance.

John didn't have to wonder anymore now that he was there. It was hard not to stare, open-mouthed, at the splendor within. But it was the priceless art collection contained within its opulent rooms that held the greatest fascination for John. Monet, Degas, Renoir, Pissarro—these were some of the artists represented on the mansion's walls..

Dinner had been an intimate affair. Only Mr. and Mrs. Palmer, Mr. and Mrs. Davenport, Miss Nordeman, and himself were present. In a dining room that seated up to fifty people, the small party had occupied the tiniest fraction of the space. Though the surroundings could have felt intimidating with their grandeur, John felt comfortable. Mr. and Mrs. Palmer were both warm and engaging hosts, without any of the pretensions one might expect of such extraordinary people.

Seated between Elizabeth and Mrs. Davenport, John couldn't help but enjoy himself throughout the long meal. Elizabeth's ease, friendliness, and humor helped him to relax, and as a conversationalist, he found her to be even more engaging than she usually was within the confines of work. The green velvet evening gown she wore matched the color of her eyes, which seemed to sparkle and dance as she spoke. John could hardly take his eyes off her.

After a main course of duck confit, the group enjoyed a dessert of a rich chocolate type of cake with port. "These are called brownies," Mrs. Palmer said. "This recipe was conceived by the kitchen staff at the Palmer House. I wanted them to create something special to commemorate the Colombian Exposition. Tell me what you think."

John agreed with everyone else in the room —they were delicious.

After dinner was over, Mrs. Palmer led the ladies to the parlor, while the men stayed behind. Mr. Palmer opened a Cuban cigar box, held out by the footman. He motioned for the others to choose one, then passed around a lighter. "Mrs. Palmer was in Europe earlier this year, and she bought so many new paintings that we needed to have a gallery built to house them all. I hear you're an artist, Mr. Lewis." Mr. Palmer stopped and let out a puff of smoke. "Marshall Field snatched you right out of art school, right? Smart fellow. We can take a stroll over to the gallery before we rejoin the ladies, and you can take a peek if you're interested."

"I'd be very interested—thank you," John said.

"Good—good, I'd like to get your opinion on the setup." Mr. Palmer rose and began heading toward the door. "Come with me, fellows."

Many of the paintings were in frames, leaning against the wall, still waiting to be hung, but John appreciated what he was seeing. Actually, he was awestruck. The Palmer's had one of the most significant art collections in all of America. And to think, Mr. Palmer was asking for his advice on how to display it? John couldn't quite believe this was happening.

After the men had finished viewing the art and had rejoined the ladies in the sitting room, Elizabeth played the piano for the group while her friend, Catherine, turned the pages of the sheet music. She performed Chopin's nocturne beautifully. He wanted to know everything there was to know about this enchanting woman. When Elizabeth finished playing, she looked up, caught John's eyes, and smiled.

Over a game of whist, a while later, Mr. Palmer brought up the topic of George Ferris's Great Wheel. "You're responsible for the window displays at Marshall Field's, Mr. Lewis, correct? I liked what you did with that model of the wheel. It was brilliant."

John glanced up just in time to see the look of disappointment flash across Elizabeth's face at hearing Mr. Palmer's praise. "That window was Miss Nordeman's idea," John said. "She's been doing some work at the store."

Instantly, Mr. Field's warning to keep Elizabeth's work at the store quiet came back to him —but it was too late. That information couldn't be retracted.

"Oh? Really? That's wonderful," Mr. Palmer said, nodding his approval toward Elizabeth. She seemed pleased by his compliment and not all concerned about John's slip of the tongue. *Maybe Mr. Field was wrong.*

By the time the evening's festivities had drawn to an end, John had forgiven himself for saying anything out of turn.   The three-story Italianate-style hall they stood in while gathering their outerwear was magnificent. Above them, moonlight poured in through the glass dome.

"Mr. Lewis, we have room in our sleigh. You may catch a ride with us," Elizabeth said, slipping on her hat.

"Thank you," John said. He didn't want his time with Elizabeth to end.

The group said their goodbyes to the Palmers and thanked them for their hospitality. Outside, the Nordeman's horse-drawn sleigh was waiting, and they all settled in for a cozy ride.

John enjoyed the feeling of sitting so close to Elizabeth. She was near enough that he noticed her perfume smelled like lily of the valley. The snow on the streets and rooftops gave the city the appearance of a frosted cake. Everything about the evening had been perfect and Chicago had never looked more beautiful to him than it did tonight.

***

"John, I have something I want to talk to you about. Meet me in front of the store at noon today, and we'll go to my club," Mr. Field said, while standing in the doorway of John's office.

John glanced up from his ledgers and nodded. "Sure, I'll be there."

Christmas was in a few days, and the store was extra busy. Mr. Field seemed to be in a good mood, and who could blame him? The sales figures were looking fantastic. So, what could Mr. Field possibly want to discuss? Hopefully, John was finally getting his long overdue raise.

Elizabeth was probably working in the studio today. Now would be a good time to put the ledgers aside and see what needed to be done downstairs. Taking one last swig of coffee, John stood, pushed his chair under his desk, and left his office.

As he passed through the retail floors, he smiled. The Christmas trees added a festive touch, and the scent of citrus and the balsam fir wafted through the air. To top it off, they had a pianist playing Christmas carols for the shoppers.

John walked into the studio and found Elizabeth singing "Joy to the World" as she tied a red bow around a vase. When she looked up, her cheeks turned a bright shade of pink. "Oh! I thought I was alone." She laughed. "You caught me singing. How are you?"

"Don't stop on account of me. You sounded great." The easy rapport they'd shared had been missing for a few weeks, but now, John was glad to have felt its return since the evening at the Palmer's. For a while, it had felt like Elizabeth had been avoiding him.

Poking a red rose into place, Elizabeth eyed John and smiled. "You know, I've been meaning to ask you something. Would you like to accompany my father and me to the fairgrounds one of these days to take a look at the Great Wheel up close? My father knows Mr. Ferris, and he offered to arrange a meeting between us—if you're interested. Apparently, Mr. Ferris quite enjoyed your tribute to his wheel with the window display." Elizabeth paused and gave John a mischievous wink. "I promise, I won't tell him that you don't think his wheel will work."

The idea of spending time with Elizabeth again, outside of work, was appealing. Plus, meeting Mr. Ferris was a privilege he didn't want to turn down. "Well, that's an offer I don't think I can refuse!"

"Okay, then. We'll make it happen." Elizabeth added water to a clean vase. "I met your brother last week. He looks a lot like you. How nice that you'll have family here with you for Christmas."

Horace hadn't mentioned that he'd met Elizabeth, but then again, John hadn't seen very much of his brother lately. Between courting Mary Peterson, who was now his fiancé, and spending a lot of time with Stuart, he was often gone when John returned to his apartment in the evenings.

John had heard rumblings about some of the delivery drivers at the store trying to organize into a union. Mr. Field wouldn't like that. Stuart Peterson's name was being tossed about as the alleged ringleader. Even a whiff of gossip about the store's workers forming unions made its way upstairs to Mr. Field, certain people would lose their jobs. Horace's close association with Stuart could cause problems if he wasn't careful. But then again, Horace would be going back to the farm in the spring, anyhow.

"Oh? I'm glad you met him. Yes, he looks like me, but we're very different. I'm the black sheep of the family. He's the favored one." John laughed. It was true, though it didn't bother him. Horace was the ideal son, as far as his family was concerned. He was carrying on the tradition of farming, and his tastes were more suited to country life. John's family loved him—but he wasn't sure they understood him.

Elizabeth laughed. "You? A black sheep? I can't see that." She loaded some of the finished floral arrangements into a box, preparing to take them upstairs. It seemed like a heavy load for such a petite woman.

"Here, I'll help you carry those upstairs," John said. "When we move over to the annex, you'll be able to use the elevator. It will be much more convenient."

"Will it?" Elizabeth teased.

John guessed she was thinking about their long confinement in the broken elevator earlier that fall. He laughed. There was no doubt in John's mind—the best days at work were those when Elizabeth was around.

***

It wasn't until after they were finished eating lunch, and the waiter had brought coffee to the table, that Mr. Field revealed the purpose of that day's meeting with John.

"Mr. Lewis, the work you've been doing at the store has gone above and beyond my high expectations. Not many are capable of that. I want you to know, I've noticed. You're going to receive that pay raise you've had coming—after the New Year, as you'll be taking on more responsibility with the opening of our annex."

"Thank you, sir. I appreciate it."

"There's one more thing. I talked to Palmer Potter, and he and I have both agreed to sponsor your nomination for membership at this club. There will be a review process. Your name will go in an open book, and all members will be able to have a say—but I don't anticipate any problems. Your star is rising, son, and you'll need the proper connections. A membership here will help."

Everything he'd been working toward over the last few years was finally starting to happen for John. "I'm deeply honored, sir. Again, thank you." What else was there to say? Words were inadequate.

"It's quite all right. Mr. Palmer seemed quite impressed with you. And you know, if you have Palmer on your side, you've got it made." Mr. Field finished his coffee and put down his cup. "I need to speak to someone here before we go back to the store. I'll be just a moment. Excuse me," Mr. Field said as he put his napkin on the table. Then he strode off, leaving John to finish his coffee alone and reflect on all the good news he'd received in one morning.

John leaned back in his chair and looked around. The richly appointed dining room at the Union League Club was filled with prominent leaders of the city. *Am I really going to be includ-*

ed as one of them? Though he was pleased that Mr. Palmer and Mr. Field were backing him, their support meant the possibility of gaining the favor of someone whose opinion mattered even more to John—Cornelius Nordeman. Elizabeth's father was the man he needed on his side. One of these days, he was going to ask him for Elizabeth's hand in marriage.

"You aren't very bright, are you? I thought I told you to stay away from Miss Nordeman." Harold Pierce had interrupted John's happy thoughts. He sat, uninvited, in the chair Mr. Field had vacated. He was staring, menacingly, at John. "And now I hear, you have her working at your store? Like some common shop girl?" He spit out the words.

"I also know you're trying to gain membership to this club. I'll blackball you, you know. I don't even need a reason." Harold clenched his hand into a tight fist on top of the table in John's view. "Cease all contact with her immediately— or not only will I make sure you never set foot in this club again, but I'll also make sure your boss knows what your brother has been up to. I hear he's been involved with the unions lately. What would that do to your career if Mr. Field knew about that—hmmm?" Harold snuffed his cigarette out on a plate, then he stood. Before he walked away, he glared at John one last time, his lip curling in a sneer. "I won't warn you again."

CHAPTER FOURTEEN

Elizabeth and Catherine were seated in the lobby at the Palmer House. Catherine's husband, Harry, was outside on the sidewalk, supervising, as the luggage was loaded onto the sleigh. The Davenports had a train to catch back to New York. The fact that Elizabeth had chosen to see her friend off here, in a public place, rather than upstairs in the apartment, was no mere coincidence. She didn't like goodbyes—and she didn't want to cry—which is what she was dangerously close to doing right now. Knowing it would be easier to maintain her composure here, among strangers, Elizabeth had suggested they meet in the sitting area by the big Tiffany clock.

"Will you be in Newport this summer?" Catherine asked. The two friends had both made their society debuts there, only a little more than two years ago. So much had changed since then.

Elizabeth answered with a shake of her head. "I don't think so—not unless it's just my mother and me who go. The Columbian Exposition starts in May. My father will be needed here in Chicago."

The Nordeman's cottage in Newport had been the place they'd gone to retreat that first year after the fire. The busy swirl of parties and balls happened without them that season. Elizabeth and her parents had kept to themselves, abstaining from any social activities, since they'd been in mourning.

"I don't think I'll be there, either. This little one will be arriving sometime around June," Catherine said, resting her hand on her still flat stomach.

Elizabeth smiled, then reached into her reticule, pulling out a small gift-wrapped package. "Here," she said, handing it to Catherine. "This is for the baby." It was a pair of soft, yellow booties she'd knitted.

"Oh, thank you, dear friend! I have something for you, too, but I left it with your mother for you to open on Christmas," Catherine said.

"I'm going to miss you, but I'm sure it will be wonderful for you and Harry to be back with your families, just in time for Christmas."

"Yes, I'll miss you too—but don't make me cry!" Catherine laughed, then put her hand on her friend's shoulder. "Elizabeth, I'm counting on seeing you again, soon. And please, don't ignore those feelings I know you have for that handsome and charming Mr. Lewis. I saw sparks between the two of you—anyone can. He's a wonderful man, and you deserve some happiness."

Elizabeth sighed, then reached for Catherine's gloved hand and squeezed it. "I like him, I'll admit that—but if he wants to pursue me, that's up to him. I'm certainly not going to chase him. So far, the only interaction I've had with him outside of work was at the Palmer's dinner party."

Harry joined the two friends in the lobby. "Well, ladies, it's time to say goodbye. The sleigh is ready."

Elizabeth stood and reached out to embrace Catherine one last time. "Send a message when you get home, so I know you arrived safely." Then she offered Harry a hug. "Enjoy your trip, and Merry Christmas. I enjoyed seeing both of you."

When all was said and done, and her friends were gone, Elizabeth drew in a deep breath and went back upstairs to her apartment. She was thinking about Catherine's words about John and what it might be like if he asked her to court him. *I would say yes— if only he asked.*

***

A few days into the New Year, over breakfast, Elizabeth's father asked her if she and Mr. Lewis were still interested in meeting with George Ferris, and Elizabeth assured him their interest hadn't waned.

"I'll send an invitation over to Mr. Lewis today." Her father cracked his boiled egg and removed the shell. "There still isn't anything to see yet of Ferris's Wheel, and it's much too cold at the Midway, anyhow—but Mr. Ferris is coming into the office tomorrow. We've got some of his architectural drawings over there. He's a busy man. But this might be your only chance to meet with him."

John had replied, saying he would be happy to come. And now, a day later, Elizabeth was in her father's office at the Rookery building, waiting for John to arrive. She was nervous, but she tried not to let it show. Meeting Mr. Ferris was the pretext, but what Elizabeth really wanted was for her father to approve of John.

From her father's tenth-floor office, Elizabeth could see the lake and a wide vista of the city. Here, they were above the coal-ash pollution that plagued the people below. Elizabeth was alone with her father for the moment. He was sitting at his desk, quietly writing something in a ledger. She looked around the office with appreciation, wishing she could come here more often.

Elizabeth liked it here. It was a place of efficiency, creativity, and industry. Quiet filled the room. The full bookcase, the sturdy mahogany desk, and the thick oriental rug on the floor all served to muffle the sounds coming from the other side of the door. Outside her father's office was a large open space with dozens of desks, most of them occupied by women, who were clicking away at typewriters—a pleasant sound to Elizabeth.

A knock and two shadows on the other side of the frosted glass alerted them. Their visitors had arrived. Elizabeth opened the door, and there stood John, next to a distinguished-looking man with a thick mustache. *This must be George Ferris.*

"Hello, we're here to see Mr. Nordeman," the mustachioed man said.

Elizabeth smiled and moved aside, welcoming both men inside. After introductions, her father offered to show everyone around the building. They took the elevator to the twelfth-floor library. Elizabeth couldn't help but think of the last time she'd been in an elevator with John. He must have been thinking the same thing too, for when she glanced at him, he gave her a wink and a smile.

Mr. Ferris was friendly and seemed happy enough to oblige her father by meeting with Elizabeth and John. "Your father has been a supporter of my project and has been a valued ally, for which I'm grateful," he said to Elizabeth. To John, he mentioned the window at Marshall Field's. "For a while there, I was starting to think that the model in your window display might be the only Great Wheel the people of Chicago were ever going to see."

John seemed to be genuinely interested in the architectural drawings that Mr. Ferris had brought along, and the two men appeared to share a connection with their mutual interest in art. Elizabeth enjoyed being in the company of these three men. Each one of them inspired her in some way.

After a pleasant hour of getting to know one another, Mr. Ferris stood to take his leave. He had another meeting upstairs with Mr. Burnham, the architect and director of the fair, in just a few minutes. "It was a pleasure to meet with you fine folks. Come and say hello this spring, when there's something to see at the Midway Plaisance. It will be spectacular. I'll be happy to show you around," Mr. Ferris said.

John stood and offered a handshake. "That would be wonderful. Thank you. I enjoyed this, and I appreciate your time, Mr. Ferris." Then John turned to Elizabeth's father. "Mr. Nordeman, thank you for your time as well, and for arranging this today. And Miss Nordeman, I thank you too."

Elizabeth thought this was the end of the meeting, and that both John and Mr. Ferris would be leaving at the same time, but after Mr. Ferris left, her father put his hand on John's shoulder and turned to his daughter. "Elizabeth, dear, why don't you find the kitchen at the end of the hallway and bring us some coffee?" Then he looked at John. "Do you have a few more minutes to stay and talk?"

John nodded. "Yes, I'd be happy to, sir."

Elizabeth left in search of the kitchen. What did her father wanted to talk to John about—and why he'd asked her to get the coffee? Usually, one of the secretaries did that sort of thing.

When she returned to the office carrying a tray with three coffee cups, Elizabeth set it on her father's desk next to the vase of white roses she'd brought in for her father earlier that morning. The men were talking about the recent cold weather the city was having. Boring. After a few minutes, John stood to excuse himself. It was time for him to get back to the store.

After John left, her father gathered some papers from his desk and placed them in a folder. "Elizabeth, would you like to stay at the office for the rest of the day, or would you like me to send for a carriage to take you home now?"

"I'd like to stay here if you don't mind. Could we please go downstairs and get something to eat, though?" Elizabeth wanted to get her father's thoughts about the morning, and in particular, on John.

Later on, when they were both enjoying hot bowls of chicken noodle soup in the lunchroom, Elizabeth listened as her father offered his opinion on John. "As I said, he's a nice fellow. I like him,but he's a bit of a *bohemian*, though, don't you think?"

"He's an artist—but no, I don't think he's bohemian. He's traditional. He works in an office, like you, and he's ambitious." The last thing Elizabeth needed was for her father to think John was a bohemian. Coming from her father, that word was *not* a compliment.

CHAPTER FIFTEEN

On Sunday morning, John woke early. His brother was sprawled out on the davenport, under a blanket, snoring loudly. The one-room apartment had been sufficient when John was the only occupant, but after Horace's arrival, it was definitely feeling more cramped. The situation was only temporary, though, and John was okay with living frugally for now. *If all goes well, I'll be buying a home soon.*

Mass was in two hours. *Maybe Horace will come today.* John poured a handful of ground coffee beans into the coffee pot and waited while they steeped. He reached into the icebox and found a package of bacon. Soon the apartment was filled with the sound of sizzling bacon and the aroma of breakfast. Horace remained motionless under his blanket, not three feet away from the stove. *He must be extra tired.* He hadn't even heard his brother come in last night. He'd already been asleep for hours.

When the bacon and coffee were ready, John started to move some papers off the table. There was a pamphlet from The American Federation of Labor amongst them. It wasn't his pamphlet, so it must have been Horace's. John had heard of the group. They fought mostly for worker's rights and fair pay—both causes John sympathized with—though he kept those feelings to himself.

He perused the pamphlet with curiosity as he sipped his coffee. Harold Pierce's threats replayed in his mind. Until now, John figured Harold had been lying about Horace's involvement with the union. But how did Harold know? Was Horace a part of this group? Now he wasn't sure.

Marshall Field fired any employee who was caught associating with union sympathizers. If Horace was found engaging in union activities, John's job would also be in jeopardy. John had been the one to vouch for Horace when he'd been hired. Heat swept through his body. He wadded up the pamphlet and threw it into the fireplace.

In spite of Harold's threats, John was prepared to risk it all for Elizabeth. Today was the day he was going to ask Cornelius Nordeman if he could court his daughter—or at least he'd write the letter.

Harold could blackball him at the Union League Club if he wanted, but he would need at least two more club members to join him to be successful in blocking John's membership. With Potter Palmer and Marshall Field sponsoring him, that wasn't likely to happen. If Harold had proof of Horace's union activities, and he followed through on his threat, John would be unemployed, and his reputation ruined. Any hope of marrying Elizabeth Nordeman would be gone forever.

Maybe I'm overreacting. Possessing a pamphlet doesn't mean my brother is actually participating in anything that will get us in trouble. Calm down. Ask Horace what he's been up to—it could be nothing.

"Horace, wake up. Come to mass with me today," John said, pulling the blanket off of his brother. He'd ask his questions on the walk there.

Horace sat up, groggy. "What time is it?"

"Nine-ten."

"Oh! I told Mary I'd be there today. I didn't realize it was so late." Horace stood, rubbing his eyes. "Hold on. I'll be ready in a minute." He poured himself a cup of coffee and gulped it down.

A few minutes later, the brothers were outside, walking briskly toward the cathedral. John pushed his hands deep into his pockets, bracing himself against the cold. Horace's face could hardly be seen. A scarf covered all but his eyes. John was in no mood to pussyfoot around the matter. "I saw the pamphlet you left on the table. Are you working with the union?"

"Oh, that? Not really. I went to one meeting with Stuart Peterson. But I'm only here for another two weeks, so I don't have time to get involved, much as I'd like to."

"Stuart Peterson? Huh. I should have warned you," John said. "Stuart knows better, though. I'll talk to him. He could lose his job if Marshall Field catches wind of this. Don't let anyone know you went to that meeting. I vouched for you. And watch yourself. If the wrong people find out you were at that meeting, both of us could lose our jobs. This is serious business, Horace."

"You know, what they're asking for is only fair," Horace said as they drew close to the church.

"That's not the point. Please, listen to me. It's important. I've got a good job—and I want to keep it!"

"Okay, brother. I hear you." Horace took his scarf off, revealing a grin. "It wouldn't be the end of the world if you lost that job. You could come back to Wisconsin and work on the farm with me."

Horace was teasing, but John didn't think it was funny. He'd worked too hard to get where he was, and he didn't want to go back to Wisconsin. John loved living in Chicago. To make his point, he gave Horace a not-too-light punch on the arm, then quickly moved away to avoid any retaliation.

Once they were inside the cathedral, John felt better. It was a peaceful place, and the organ music was soothing. It suddenly seemed harder to imagine why he had been upset about his brother's activities.

Elizabeth sat between her parents, a few rows in front of him, on the other side of the room. She looked beautiful. Her presence calmed him. John wouldn't delay any longer. He would speak to Mr. Nordeman about his daughter at the earliest opportunity. It also wouldn't hurt to pray first.

***

Mrs. Sanders had finished the wedding dress John had requested for the window display. He had dropped by the sewing studio that morning to check on its progress and had been pleased to see the beautiful silk gown hanging on a rack near the back wall.

"Mrs. Sanders, you've outdone yourself. It's exquisite. When this dress goes in the window, women all over the city will be asking for you to make their wedding dresses. I hope you're ready to be busy," John said admiringly, as he ran his fingers over the delicate pearl beadwork.

Mrs. Sanders blushed. "I just copied the drawing you made. You designed it, sir. But that dress was a thorn in my side. Oh, my. It was difficult. I'm not sure I want to sew another wedding dress anytime soon!" But her smile revealed she was proud of the dress and rightly so. "I made a veil to go with it." The older woman shuffled over to another rack and found the piece, then brought it over to John.

"Thank you. This is perfect. I'm excited to see the window when it's all put together."

John excused himself after instructing an assistant to have the dress and veil brought to the staging area on the main floor. The stained glass window was already there, ready and waiting. His next plan was to visit the basement studio and talk to Elizabeth. He'd need her help with the fresh flower arrangements.

As John took the steps down toward the basement, he thought about the letter he'd sent to Mr. Nordeman on Monday morning. Today was Tuesday. Had he received it yet? John had put it all on the line. If he'd misread Elizabeth, and she didn't return his feelings toward her, or if her father refused to let the relationship go any further, John would still need to continue working with her—and it would be awkward.

Would Mr. Nordeman speak to Elizabeth first before giving him an answer? The question made John feel more nervous the closer he got to the studio. He decided to proceed as if nothing were different until he either heard back from Mr. Nordeman, or Elizabeth brought it up, whichever came first.

"Good morning, John," Elizabeth said when John entered the studio. She looked up from the vase in front of her and smiled. She seemed perfectly relaxed, giving no indication of any knowledge of the letter.

"Good morning!" John greeted her, trying his best to match her tone. He would follow her lead. "I need a large arrangement of flowers for the right corner window facing State Street by tomorrow. Would that be something you could do by then? It's a wedding display. Remember that stained glass window I was working on? I'll be using that, and Mrs. Sanders made a beautiful gown."

"Oh, it all sounds lovely! I love that piece—
it's a work of art. And yes, I can put together an
arrangement. What color do you want?"

John pulled out his sketches to show Elizabeth what he had in mind, and they decided together that various shades of pink and purple
would be best. As they talked, it was hard for
John not to think of Elizabeth wearing the beautiful gown that would be going in the window—
but he put an end to those thoughts as quickly as
he could. *It won't do any good to get ahead of
yourself.*

It wasn't until lunchtime that John left the
studio again. He decided to stop by the loading
dock and see if Horace and Stuart were there
and if they wanted to grab a quick bite to eat
with him. Horace was unhitching a team of
horses when John found him. John waited while
his brother finished up. When Horace walked
over, John asked if Stuart was around.

"No, Stuart isn't here." Horace appeared
somber. "I was going to come and find you, but
you came here first. I need to talk to you."

"What about?" John was confused.

"I'll tell you over lunch," Horace said.

"Is everything okay?" John didn't need to wait for a reply to get his answer. His brother was clearly upset.

Over a lunch of pastrami on rye in John's office upstairs, Horace spoke in a hushed tone. "Stuart was called up to Mr. Field's office this morning. He didn't come back afterward. Several other men were sent upstairs too. None of them came back, so now we're short-handed on delivery drivers. All of them were at that union meeting we went to. The rumor is, they were all fired. Some people think there's a snitch who ratted everyone out."

John's heart beat faster in his chest. It was what he had feared. "But they didn't call you?"

"No, not yet."

"Maybe, they won't." John was trying to be hopeful. These were rumors. There could be another explanation for why Stuart and the men didn't come back to work that morning. Yet, it felt like a dark cloud had blown over them.

Horace looked down at his hands. "If I'm called to Mr. Field's office, I'll tell the truth. You didn't have anything to do with it. And don't worry about Stuart. Before any of this even happened, he was already talking about moving to Wisconsin when Mary and I are married. He's tired of the city, Matilda broke it off with him, and I could use his help on the farm. But Mr. Field likes you. You shouldn't have anything to worry about."

John wanted to believe his brother. But John knew his boss. Ever since the Haymarket Riots, Mr. Field had taken a hard line against unions. He wasn't as confident that his job was secure. Harold Pierce wouldn't even need to follow through on those threats he'd made. It looked like the worst possible scenario would happen anyway—without Harold's interference.

CHAPTER SIXTEEN

The lamplighters were already igniting the streetlamps when Elizabeth's carriage dropped her off in front of the Palmer House. She'd stayed late at work, getting the flowers ready for John's new window. He'd seemed distracted after lunch. The first floral arrangement Elizabeth made for the window display was destroyed—an unfortunate mishap on the stairwell.

While transporting it upstairs to the staging area, John had dropped the vase. It shattered into thousands of tiny pieces. They'd salvaged what flowers they could, and Elizabeth had started again on a second one. John was apologetic and seemingly embarrassed. Elizabeth had done her best to minimize the situation by remaining calm. She'd been more concerned about John's distress than the extra work it had caused her.

Now that she was home, Elizabeth regretted not sending a message ahead to her parents, letting them know she'd be late. Upon entering the apartment, she immediately made her way to her mother's bedroom, where she'd be getting ready for dinner.

Elizabeth's mother was seated at the dressing table, looking through her jewelry box. "Have you been at the store all this time?" She held up a pair of drop pearl earrings and considered them.

"I have. I'm sorry, I'm late. I'll be ready in time for dinner. I just wanted to let you know I was back," Elizabeth said. "Did you have a nice day?"

"I did, thank you. Your father has something he wants to talk to you about after dinner."

"Oh? Do you know what it's about?" Elizabeth picked up her mother's bottle of Bouquet de Violette and gave a spritz to her wrist.

"I can't say. Go, get dressed. You'll find out soon enough."

After dinner, the family gathered together in the library. The fire was crackling, the lamps were dim, and the room felt cozy. Elizabeth had put a record on the phonograph player. They were listening to Charles K. Harris sing "After the Ball."

Father sat back in his favorite green velvet wingback chair by the fireplace and closed his eyes as if he was going to take a nap. Elizabeth grew impatient. She tried to focus on her needlepoint work. *If he has something he wants to talk to me about, why doesn't he get to it?*

Finally, after a few more minutes, her father opened his eyes, cleared his throat, and reached into his front jacket pocket. He pulled out a letter, then got straight to the point. "John Lewis wrote to me." He looked at Elizabeth. "He wants my permission to court you."

Elizabeth couldn't hide the smile that immediately came to her face. "What is your reply?"

"I have my reservations." Her father raised both eyebrows. "But I can see how much the idea pleases you."

"What do we know about his family?" Mother asked as she put down the book she'd been reading.

"His family is from Wisconsin." Elizabeth moved closer to her mother. "They're farmers—but so was Father. John speaks fondly of them. They're good people. I've met his brother." Then she turned to her father. "And yes, the idea pleases me a great deal."

He nodded. Her father seemed to be carefully considering his next words. "Marshall Field and Potter Palmer recently sponsored Mr. Lewis's membership at the Union League Club, I hear. They must see something in him too. It wouldn't hurt, I suppose, to allow a trial—if that's what you want, Elizabeth."

Elizabeth glanced at her mother, who gave the slightest shake of her head, yet she remained quiet.   Mother's reaction was understandable. She would have preferred for her daughter to be matched with someone who came from equal or greater wealth. It was simply the way things were done.

Her mother sighed. "What about his faith? Is he Catholic?"

"He is. I've seen him at Holy Name a few times." Elizabeth didn't know much beyond that, but she figured that was the whole point of courting. She'd learn these things, and they would get to know each other better over time.

Her father stood and walked to the window, gazing out to the street below. It was snowing again. "I'll let Mr. Lewis know he may call on you, but your mother and I will be watching closely."

"Thank you." Elizabeth moved to where her father was standing and reached up to kiss him on the cheek. After that, she excused herself and went to her bedroom to retire for the evening.

When Sissy came into Elizabeth's room to help her out of her evening gown and into her nightclothes, Elizabeth felt like she was floating on a cloud. "Sissy, John Lewis finally asked my father if he could call on me."

Sissy smiled as she slipped Elizabeth's dress on a hanger. "That's wonderful, Miss. I can see how happy that makes you."

Was there a special man in Sissy's life? Her maid had come with the family from New York. *She probably doesn't even have time. She's always working.* That was a sad thought.

Sissy took Elizabeth's gown and carefully hung it up in the wardrobe before saying goodnight. It was with great relief when Elizabeth finally crawled into her large four-poster featherbed and sank back onto the pillows. But it was a long time before she fell asleep that night. There were a lot of questions to ponder. *Does John even know that if he were to marry me, he'd eventually need to take over my father's business? Will he want to? And if he doesn't? I'm not going to think about that.*

She thought he seemed out of sorts. The memory of the broken vase on the stairwell, the scattered flowers, and John's distress played itself over in Elizabeth's mind. He must have already sent the letter to Father by that time. It seemed like something was bothering him. Elizabeth hoped he didn't already have regrets.

***

"My brother and Mary Peterson are getting married on Saturday morning at City Hall," John said. "Afterward, her brother, Stuart, is throwing a small party for them at Bailey's restaurant before they leave for Wisconsin. Would you like to come?" For the last week, he'd stopped by several times after work to visit Elizabeth at her home. Elizabeth's parents usually hovered nearby, but still, she enjoyed being with John in this new context.

"A Valentine's wedding? How romantic! Yes—and thank you. I'd love to come. So, they're going back to Wisconsin?"

"Yes, and Stuart is going with them. My parents have been taking care of the farm all winter, but they're getting older and keeping up with the work isn't as easy for them as it used to be. It's time for Horace to get back and start the spring work."

Annette, the housekeeper, came into the room for what must have been the fifth time in the past hour. This time she brought a tray with tea and set it in front of the couple. Elizabeth's parents were at a dinner party tonight, so she and John were alone—though it was evident that Annette had been given instructions to serve as a sort of chaperone for the evening.

John went over to the upright piano and touched the keys. "Do you mind if I play something?"

"Please, do." Elizabeth poured herself a cup of tea and sat back to listen as John began to play "Mazurka" by Chopin from memory. As the beautiful music filled the room, Elizabeth thought about how this was just one more wonderful surprise to learn about this man she was starting to fall in love with.

After a while, Elizabeth went and sat next to John on the piano bench. He was so close, and she noticed the faintest whiff of cedarwood from his cologne.

When he finished the song, John smiled. "I haven't played in a long while. There isn't room for a piano in my apartment. I guess I've missed it. Do you know any duets?"

She did. For the next hour, Elizabeth and John played every piece of sheet music available in the apartment that was written for two. The feeling of his hands, brushing against hers, the emotion with which John played, and the obvious enjoyment he had for the music, was irresistible to Elizabeth. It was a perfect evening, and she didn't want it to end.

***

On Saturday, Elizabeth and John rode the street-car to City Hall with Horace, Stuart, and Mary. Elizabeth looked over at Mary and realized that it was the first time she'd seen the woman wearing anything but the black skirt and white shirt-waist uniform used by every woman who worked at Marshall Field's. But today, Mary was wearing a smart black bonnet trimmed with a pink ribbon, and a brown wool cape, decorated with the same ribbon. In her hands, she held a bouquet of red roses and white carnations that Elizabeth had given her. The bride was pretty and seemed very happy.

Earlier, Elizabeth had asked John why no parents would be attending the ceremony. She couldn't imagine getting married without her mother and father present. John told her that Mr. and Mrs. Peterson had both died a few years ago during the flu pandemic, and John and Horace's parents were not up to traveling such a long distance. It was the only sad part of an otherwise joyous occasion.

The ceremony was brief and simple. Horace and Mary said their vows in front of a judge. They were two people who were obviously in love, and it was sweet. Elizabeth considered it a special honor to witness such a blessed event. It was a short walk over to Bailey's after the judge pronounced Horace and Mary to be man and wife.

Inside the restaurant, the atmosphere was lively. The noise level was high, and smoke filled the room. A phonograph player in the corner provided upbeat music. A group of young men at a table nearby were laughing loudly and eating sausages and fried potatoes. The inviting smell made Elizabeth feel hungry. Bailey's was like no place she'd visited before, and she liked it.

Stuart ordered a round of drinks for the group. "A toast to love, laughter, and happily ever after," he said as he raised his glass.

Mary, who was the frankest person Elizabeth had ever met, admitted over lunch that she'd disliked Elizabeth at first, but she added that it wasn't personal, and Elizabeth shouldn't worry. "I was jealous because I wanted John to notice me, but ever since you came along, he's only had eyes for you. It worked out in the end, though." Mary laughed. "I love Horace! And you? You surprised me, Elizabeth. You're much more fun than I expected. I wonder if we'll be sisters one day!"

Elizabeth laughed at that, and she could feel her face turning a bright shade of pink—especially when John looked over, smiled, and gave her a wink.

Elizabeth had her own reasons for feeling envious of Mary, but she didn't admit them out loud. The teasing, affectionate relationship she observed between Mary and her brother, Stuart, reminded Elizabeth of how it had been with her own brother, Samuel. It made her miss him.

After lunch, it was time for goodbyes. Horace, Mary, and Stuart had a train to catch. The three of them took a Hansom cab to the station, leaving John and Elizabeth to walk back to the Palmer House on their own.

"I had fun today. Thank you for inviting me," Elizabeth said as she placed her hand in the crook of John's bent arm.

"I did too. I thought I'd be happy to have my place all to myself again, but I think I'm going to miss my brother."

Elizabeth could hardly feel her frozen toes, and the icy wind stung the exposed skin on her face, but she was happy to be with John. They walked quickly back to the Palmer House.

The hotel's lobby felt warm and inviting. Instead of going to Elizabeth's apartment, they chose to sit in her favorite chairs by the big clock. Even though people were coming and going all around them, they were still afforded more privacy here than under her mother's watchful eye.

John told Elizabeth about how Stuart, Horace, and several other employees at Marshall Field's had been fired for their involvement with the unions. "I thought my time there had come to an end too—simply because of my relation to Horace. But I wasn't involved, and I guess Mr. Field knows that's the truth, because I still have my job." John paused. "That day I dropped the vase—I was waiting to hear if I'd be fired. I'd also just sent a letter to your father, asking if I could call on you. That felt like the longest day ever."

Elizabeth tried to make the question sound casual. "Do you like your job?"

"Very much—though I don't agree with what happened to those men who went to the union meeting. I wish I could get them their jobs back. But I enjoy what I do. When I first moved to Chicago, I didn't quite know how I would make a living and be an artist at the same time. Visual Merchandising allows me to do that. I feel very fortunate to be where I am."

Elizabeth nodded and stood. Something about the conversation was making her feel uncomfortable. It was time to start getting ready for dinner. "I should probably go back upstairs now. Would you like to sit with my family at mass tomorrow morning?"

"I'll walk you upstairs—and yes, I would like that. Thank you," John said.

In the hallway, outside her family's apartment, Elizabeth paused. She wanted John to kiss her. For too long now, she'd imagined what it would be like to feel his lips on her own. He was standing so close, and it seemed like he wanted to kiss her too.

Elizabeth waited. She looked up into his deep blue eyes. *My word, he's handsome.* Finally, Elizabeth moved toward him, intending to kiss him on the cheek. Instead, he pulled her closer and kissed her on the mouth—gentle, loving, and slow. *This feels perfect.*

After he pulled away, John smiled. "Happy Valentine's Day, sweet Elizabeth." He lowered his voice to a whisper. "I love you." Before he turned to go, he handed her a letter. "I express my feelings better in writing."

Elizabeth smiled and took the envelope, though she thought he'd just expressed his feelings more than adequately.

CHAPTER SEVENTEEN

The conversation at the Nordeman's dinner party on Friday evening centered around art, music, and travel—safe topics. John wished he had been seated closer to Elizabeth, but he pushed that thought away as he reminded himself how much he had to be grateful for. At least now, he was at the same table, even if he could only admire her beauty from across the room.

It was preferable to what he'd had until a month prior, when he'd only seen Elizabeth in passing moments, and solely within the context of work. Tonight, he was seated between Mrs. Palmer and Mrs. Caton. Mrs. Palmer was an entertaining conversationalist, and John appreciated the warmth with which she'd accepted him into her circle.

The constraints that came with courting Elizabeth Nordeman were extensive. The high society world she inhabited was one of strict protocols and expectations. But John was a quick student—one who easily adapted to the norms and standards expected of him. In John's mind, abiding by these rules was but a small price to pay for the pleasure of her company.

After dessert, Mrs. Nordeman stood, and the other five ladies followed her out the door. John was looking forward to joining Elizabeth in the sitting room later. But first, there would be the customary cigars, port, and political talk with the men who were left behind in the dining room. It would be a long while, however, before John got his wish. The men had a lot they wanted to talk about.

"Did you hear the news about the Philadelphia and Reading Railroad today?" Mr. Nordeman asked. "Bankrupt." He poured himself a glass of port from a crystal bottle.

The other men nodded. It must have been on all their minds. "We could see something like '73 all over again. It's a similar situation. Mark my word. This is just the beginning," Mr. Palmer said.

John declined the cigar Mr. Nordeman offered and listened to the others. He didn't want what they were saying to be true. A somber mood fell over the room. John was only a boy in '73, but he remembered that year. His father had to sell Gretel, his horse. They'd actually sold most of the farm's animals, trying to come up with enough money to pay off a debt that the bank had suddenly recalled.

He loved that horse, and he cried when the man came to take her away. His father was sorry about the loss, and he'd explained they didn't have a choice. They had to sell the animals, or the bank would take the whole farm over.

That same year, his school closed. The community couldn't afford to pay the teacher. It was then that John decided he didn't want to be a farmer. A while later, he set his sights on Chicago, a city he'd equated with wealth, and began planning to leave Belmont, Wisconsin, as soon as he could. Subsequently, John learned people all over the country had faced significant losses that year—some, far worse.

Right now, all of the money John had been saving for a home over the past few years was in the bank. If Mr. Palmer was correct about his prediction, and if banks started failing, he could lose everything. Now was the time for him to get his money out and buy a house. John decided to start looking.

***

A house on Prairie Avenue, where many of Chicago's most fashionable homes were located, was too far out of reach for John. Though he had a sizable nest egg, he needed to be realistic. He'd search for a home in the recently annexed community of Englewood, near the fairgrounds and the omnibus line. It would still be easy to get to work downtown. Here, upwind from the stockyards, the air was cleaner, and the homes were pretty, yet modest enough for middle-class families to attain. At least, John hoped this was still the case. Real estate prices were rising all over the city because of the upcoming exposition.

John thought about the Nordeman's luxury apartment at the Palmer House as he walked down Halstead Street. He wanted to provide the same lifestyle for Elizabeth that she was accustomed to, and he believed he would—someday. But for now, Englewood was like an excellent place to start. John had the name of a lawyer, Mr. Hayes, and an address scribbled on a piece of paper. Mr. Hayes would be able to show John some houses that were available in the neighborhood—as soon as John found his office.

A few minutes later, John entered a two-story, red brick office building under a sign that read, *Glenn Hayes, Attorney at Law*. A tinkling bell above the door announced his arrival. The tiny room housed a messy desk stacked with piles of books, behind which sat an older gentleman of immense proportions. The man had a face reminiscent of a bulldog.

"What can I do for you?" the man asked gruffly, still holding a smoking pipe in his mouth.

After a brief introduction and an explanation for the reason behind John's visit, Mr. Hayes offered a chair, and the two men began discussing the necessary details. When the nitty-gritty of what John could afford to spend came up, Mr. Hayes leaned back in his chair and shook his head.

"That might have gotten you a house here a few years ago, but not anymore. Investors are snapping up everything available so they can rent out the rooms during the fair. You're going to need more money than that."

John felt defeated. He didn't know what to do. "Are you sure there's nothing?"

Mr. Hayes softened his expression. "Do you have good credit? Some banks will lend up to fifty percent of the cost of a home. You might consider something like that."

John thought about the loan his father had taken out to pay for the home he'd built his family in Belmont. It was a risky move. When the bank had demanded the full payment before the agreed-upon time, John's father had nearly lost everything. It wasn't a position John wanted to put himself in. "I'll look into my options."

The meeting was over. John thanked Mr. Hayes and shook his hand. After that, he wandered around Englewood, admiring the neat lawns and tidy homes. It was the kind of place that seemed perfect to raise a family. Would Elizabeth think so too? Maybe it wouldn't hurt to at least talk to a banker.

***

John was having lunch with Marshall Field in the dining room at the club on Monday when he looked up and saw Harold Pierce watching them from across the room. Harold, who was alone at the bar, had a sour expression on his face.

Mr. Field noticed him too. "Watch your back around that one," he said. "Did I tell you Mr. Pierce came to my office a few weeks ago? He wanted to talk about you—claimed you were a union sympathizer—and he thought I should know. As if I don't already know what's going on with my employees. What an insult! If you were involved with the unions, I'd be aware of it—believe me. I know you're more sensible than that. Your brother, however, is a different story. You might talk some sense into him for his own good."

Mr. Field shook his head and frowned as he took a bite of steak. "Mr. Pierce also put up a squawk about your membership nomination.

Mind you. Nobody took him seriously. Around here, we all know what he's like. You're not the first person he's spread rumors about." John's boss leaned back in his chair and studied Harold. "What'd you do to get on his bad side, anyway?"

"I'm courting Miss Nordeman, sir—and Mr. Pierce seems to think he has a claim on her. He told me he'd go to you. He wanted me to lose my job. I'm sorry you were dragged into that mess." John ignored Mr. Field's comment about his brother.

Mr. Field laughed. "Courting Miss Nordeman, huh? Good for you."

A waiter brought two dishes of chocolate ice cream to the table, and Harold was soon forgotten as the topic turned back toward what they'd been discussing before. The new annex at the store was almost ready to move into, and John needed to hire several more people to keep up with everything.

When lunch was over, John was waiting at the coat check when Harold came and stood behind him. "So, I heard you want to buy a house, and you need a loan. You're lucky your boss is a foolish man, and he let you keep your job. But you won't be so lucky when you try to get that loan. I can stop you—and I will. You'll regret not listening to me. You should have stayed away from Elizabeth Nordeman."

How does he find these things out? Though Harold's father was a powerful banker, he certainly didn't have that much power. John didn't believe Harold's bluff this time, but he said nothing. Instead, he put on his hat and coat— handed to him by the man behind the counter. Then John turned to Harold, smiled, and tipped his hat before walking out the door.

CHAPTER EIGHTEEN

E lizabeth stopped by the front desk as she was coming through the lobby and left a message for one of the bellhops to bring her bicycle upstairs. After her mother's unfortunate accident in the park, the basement storage room at the Palmer House seemed like the right place for it.

It was a warm spring day for late March, and now that the snow had melted, and the days were getting longer, Elizabeth was ready to give bicycling another try. Over dinner, the night before, Elizabeth asked her mother if she wouldn't like to go for a ride at Lake Park again. Her mother swiftly said no, but John, who'd been dining with the family, surprised Elizabeth by saying that he had a bicycle. Now, he was on his way to meet Elizabeth so they could take a ride together in the park.

Elizabeth chose to sit by the front window in the lobby while she waited for John to arrive. It was an ideal spot to observe all that was going on inside the hotel and on the street. After several months of living at the Palmer House, Elizabeth had grown to love it. The staff was dear to her, and she enjoyed the constant activity and the interesting people who came through. It was never dull. For example, at the moment, an elderly couple was checking in with two large white standard poodles wearing what appeared to be diamond studded collars.

When John came through the front entrance, Elizabeth remained where she was. He didn't see her, and she watched as he smiled and greeted people around him by name. He treated everyone equally—with kindness and respect, no matter their station in life. It was one more reason Elizabeth was so deeply attracted to him. The manner in which her parents, and others of their generation, treated servants as if they were invisible at times, had always made her uncomfortable. John turned toward her. She loved the way his eyes locked onto her, alone, from across the room. It made her feel special.

John was wearing a short jacket and knee-length trousers with long woolen socks—the attire of an experienced cyclist. Elizabeth needed to get some cycling clothes straight away.

Elizabeth stood and greeted John as he approached. "Mr. Gilbert said my bicycle is waiting for me right out front. I'm ready to go."

Soon, the two of them were at Lake Park, speeding along the pathways. The wind and sunshine felt invigorating. Elizabeth's face warmed as she exerted herself. A feeling of freedom came over her. The last time she'd rode, she'd been so concerned about her mother, that she'd missed out on all the wonderful scenery. John, who was ahead of her, looked back and smiled. Then he motioned toward a bench, indicating he wanted to stop for a rest.

Elizabeth leaned her bike against a tree and sat down on the bench with John. She was comfortable with him. "Tell me, how's your brother and Mary doing? Have you heard anything from them lately?"

"A letter came yesterday, as a matter of fact. The newlyweds are quite well, thank you, and they send their love to you." John took a piece of wrapped cheese from his pocket and offered some to Elizabeth. "Tell me about your brother. What was he like?"

Elizabeth gazed out over Lake Michigan. Sailboats bobbed about on the choppy waves. Winter hadn't let go of its grasp on the city quite yet. She reached for John's hand while thinking about her answer. His firm grasp felt warm and comforting.

"Samuel was two years older than me, and he was my best friend. He was always making me laugh. One time, when I was fifteen, my brother came to visit me at my boarding school. He wanted to take me to the circus. Mrs. Okill, the headmistress, would never have allowed such a thing, so he devised some elaborate scheme to get me out of there—something to do with a dead Aunt Clarice. I don't have an Aunt Clarice, but I went along with it.

"Somehow, I suspected it was Samuel behind the message sent to my school. We had the best time. He told me he wanted to run away with the circus and become an elephant trainer. Samuel loved animals. I told him, if one *really* loved animals, he'd want those elephants to be free, and then, he said I was right—he hadn't thought of it that way. I'll never forget that. Because he didn't usually admit when he was wrong." Elizabeth smiled as she thought about the memories. "He was going to take over our father's business..."

John didn't pry. He remained quiet as he listened. Elizabeth considered whether to say more. She'd never spoken to anyone about the night of the fire. But if John loved her, she wanted him to know the whole truth about her.

"It was my fault Samuel died." Elizabeth paused as she began to tear up.

"What makes you say that?" John asked gently.

"The whole house was filled with thick smoke when Annette, our housekeeper, woke me that night. It hurt to breathe, and everything was dark. She gave me my robe and told me to run out of the house. She told me to go out to the street, where my family would be waiting for me. I did as she said. I made it out of the house, and Annette was right. Everyone—the servants, and my family, were safe and accounted for.

"But I had a cat, and I wanted to go back in and get her. Flames were coming from the second-floor windows, but I thought I still had time. The fire wasn't in the lower levels yet. Minksy, my cat, usually slept in the kitchen. I started to run back into the house to find her, but my father held me back. I pulled myself loose and went in, anyway." Elizabeth took a deep breath and waited to get her emotions under control.

"My brother caught up with me and told me to go back outside. Samuel said he'd find Minksy for me. But he never came back out of the house. A beam fell on him. The firefighters pulled him out, but it was too late. I'll never forgive myself..." A tear slipped down Elizabeth's face, which she quickly wiped away.

John offered Elizabeth a clean handkerchief from his pocket. "I'm sorry those terrible things happened to you and your family. I think it's okay to feel regret over the events of that night—but to hold yourself responsible? That's a heavy load. I know I can't change the way you feel, but it sounds to me like there were a lot of things that were outside of your control." His compassionate gaze held hers. "I'm glad you talked to me. I'm here for you." He placed his hand over hers. "I love you."

He loved her. Elizabeth was glad he didn't try to talk her out of the way she felt. John's words let Elizabeth know she could be honest with him. His response, in a strange way, made her feel lighter. There was more she needed to tell him—but for now, it was enough.

John and Elizabeth rode their bicycles back to the Palmer House. Elizabeth handed her bike back over to the bellhop, and then she said goodbye to John. "Thank you." Such words felt so inadequate.

She leaned closer and whispered in his ear. "I love you too."

***

Elizabeth snapped the stem off of a yellow rose and pinned it onto the lapel of John's suit jacket. He'd stopped by the basement studio while she was preparing the vases for the Ladies Lounge.

"I have a meeting at the bank this morning. I just wanted to stop by and say hello, in case you're already gone when I return," John said.

"Are you coming by the apartment this evening?"

"Yes, if that's all right."

It was *more* than all right. Elizabeth's parents, though initially wary of John, had warmed up to him. They enjoyed having him stop by the apartment almost as much as she did. Her mother had eased up considerably on the restrictions she'd imposed at the beginning of John and Elizabeth's courtship.

As he put on his hat, John fumbled with a folder he was holding. Papers fell onto the floor, scattering everywhere. Elizabeth helped him gather everything back together. John laughed. "I can really be clumsy sometimes."

"We all have our clumsy moments," Elizabeth said, laughing too.

"I'll see you later. I hope you have a good day."

John left, and Elizabeth resumed working on the floral arrangements.

It wasn't until much later, when she was cleaning up, that she noticed a pamphlet on the floor under the coat tree. *That must be John's. I hope he didn't need it today.* She picked it up.

Elizabeth intended on returning the pamphlet to John's office. She wasn't trying to be nosy. It appeared to be some type of advertisement for a home in Englewood. The drawing depicted a lovely, classical greystone. Her heart started beating faster as several realizations set in. John's work at the store didn't usually involve meeting with bankers. His errand must have been personal. *Does this house have something to do with his meeting at the bank? Is he buying a home?*

Elizabeth needed to talk to John—soon. Unlike most men who wanted to court her, John didn't seem to carry any presumptions about what marriage to her would mean for his own career and fortune. Elizabeth was confident that John pursued their relationship because he was interested in her—not because he wanted to run Nordeman Insurance. *But he hasn't asked me to marry him, yet.* It was an uncomfortable situation to be in.

Slipping the pamphlet into her pocket, Elizabeth decided to give it to John when he came by the apartment later that evening. It would provide an opening to talk about some important matters.

***

At nine o' clock, Elizabeth's parents said good-night and retired to their rooms. John and Elizabeth were finally alone. John stood by the fireplace. He was looking at the family pictures on the mantel.

Elizabeth walked over to him. "Here, this is one of the papers you dropped earlier today. It was under the coat tree."

John quickly took the paper without glancing at it. He slipped it into his inner coat pocket. "Thank you."

Elizabeth tried another approach as she sat down. "How did your meeting at the bank go today?"

"Very well, thank you."

Subtlety wasn't going to work here. "Are you buying a house?"

"Yes...but I was hoping to surprise you." John sounded disappointed.

"Well, I'm glad I found out, then. We need to talk. I didn't want to bring this up so early, but I think you should know—if we were to get married, we would need to live in New York, near headquarters." She stood. "Would you like to go out to the balcony to talk?"

John nodded and followed Elizabeth outside.

"You would eventually take over Nordeman Insurance. It was supposed to go to Samuel. And now, since his death, I have a responsibility to him that I must uphold. The man I marry must be willing and able to take on that responsibility too."

John sat down quietly and looked up at the full moon. Elizabeth grew increasingly uncomfortable as his silence stretched on.

Elizabeth sat down next to him and put her hand on top of his. "I know it's a lot to take in. I've been trying to find the right way to tell you. I'm sorry."

"Your father runs his business from Chicago right now..."

"He has people in New York running the company for him, but it's temporary. He wants to keep the business in the family. He worked so hard to build it."

"You're right—this is a lot. I don't know what to say. I—I need to get my thoughts straight first. Can we talk more later?"

John's mood seemed strangely subdued to Elizabeth. The company was worth a fortune. Didn't he know this? Maybe he didn't care. Perhaps this was too much for him. And maybe it wasn't what he wanted. If so, what would Elizabeth do?

Fear, doubt, and more questions crashed about in Elizabeth's head, but outwardly, she remained composed. "Of course."

CHAPTER NINETEEN

The store still wouldn't open for another couple of hours, but John hadn't been able to sleep after his conversation with Elizabeth the night before, so he'd come in early to get a head start on dismantling the wedding display window.

It was still dark outside when John entered his office on the top floor. The sound of silence greeted him. For now, the store felt more like an old library than a bustling palace of commerce. Down the hallway, light streamed from beneath the doorway of Mr. Field's office. The distinct aroma of fresh coffee drew John closer to the door. He tapped on it.

"Come in," his boss said, and John accepted the invitation.. Mr. Field was reading the morning paper. "Pour yourself a cup of coffee. There's another mug over on that shelf."

"Thank you. I thought I might be the first person in this morning." John took a sip of coffee. "I'm switching over the wedding window to an Easter display this morning, and I wanted to get an early start."

"I'm always the first one here. That window was an attractive display, and sales in the bridal department are up. You're doing good work," Mr. Field put down his paper and gave John his full attention.

John smiled in response to the compliment. His job at the store seemed tailor-made for his particular talents, and his position wasn't something to take for granted. Saying goodbye, John left his boss's office and headed downstairs.

Leaving this place, on his own accord, had never crossed his mind—not until last night. *What do I know about the insurance business?* Elizabeth's words had surprised him. John still didn't know what to think. The questions laid heavy on his mind. Elizabeth's happiness was a high priority for John and so was keeping her in the style of comfort and luxury she was accustomed to. But John didn't know how to run a company—and he wasn't sure he wanted to. John thought of himself as an artist, not a businessman.

Elizabeth is probably more capable of running her father's company than I am. The idea made him smile. ohn remembered the first time he'd met her, when she'd come into his office, full of moxie and purpose. She'd had a business plan from the start. He'd never met another woman quite like her. He loved Elizabeth fiercely—in a way he didn't even know was possible.

Taking the wedding gown from the window off the dress form, John carefully placed it in a box lined with tissue paper. The store would sell it now. To whom? He didn't know—but John hoped it would make the bride it was destined for feel beautiful when she wore it.

To see his design come to life under the capable hands of Mrs. Sanders, the seamstress, had been thrilling. He liked designing clothes. John tried to picture what running an insurance business would be like, but he couldn't.

On the other hand, he could see as clearly as if she were standing in front of him right now— Elizabeth—as his lovely bride. *If running her family's insurance business is what it takes to marry her, then I'll do it. I just hope I'm capable.*

***

"Did Elizabeth inform you that she and her mother are going to New York next week?" Mr. Nordeman asked John. They were sharing lunch in the dining room at The Rookery. Last night, after dinner, Mr. Nordeman had asked John to come by his office in the morning.

John nodded. "She did, sir." A waiter placed a plate with squab and mashed potatoes covered in gravy in front of him.

"Patricia will be staying in the city, checking on the progress of our home that's under construction," Mr. Nordeman said after the waiter left. "Elizabeth will be visiting her friend, Mrs. Davenport, nearby in Port Chester. I want to go —but with the fair opening in less than a month, I simply can't get away. Have you ever been to New York City, son?"

"No, sir."

"The ladies will be there for a week. You should go with them." Mr. Nordeman took a bite of his dinner. "Patricia can book you a room at The Plaza. I'll send word to my office and tell them you're coming. You can go in and get a feel for the place. I'll have them to show you around. You need to know what you're signing up for. Don't you think? There's a lot you'll need to catch up on."

It had only been a few days since the conversation with Elizabeth regarding his future in the family's company. It was all moving so fast. The offer was generous and sensible. But stepping away from his work at Marshall Field's right now would cause all kinds of problems for the store. Preparations to open the new annex were in full swing, and John was needed. He felt torn.

"Sir, I would very much like to go to New York right now, and I appreciate your generous offer. However, I will have to decline. I have commitments at work that I can't, in good conscience, leave on short notice," John said.

Mr. Nordeman furrowed his brow and frowned. "I see. Tell me more about what you do at Marshall Field's."

"I'm a Visual Merchandising Director, sir. I promote the image of Marshall Field's, design the windows and in-store displays—and the interior design of the new annex is something I'm working on right now." John knew, as he was describing his job, how it must have sounded to Mr. Nordeman. John was not qualified, in any way, to run an insurance company.

"And am I correct that you do want to work for my company?" Mr. Nordeman asked.

"Yes, sir."

"And when would that be? Time is of the essence here."

Sweat around his collar made John want to loosen his tie. He felt like a bug under a microscope. He did his best to appear more confident than he felt with his response. "Sir, Mr. Field has been very good to me, and I want to treat him fairly in return. I would like to stay on and finish my commitment, up until the opening of the annex. That would be August, sir, by current estimates."

"Very well, then. I can't fault you for lack of loyalty," Mr. Nordeman said, but the disappointment on his face couldn't be missed. .

***

Inside the Nordeman's private Pullman car, John watched as the countryside changed from flat plains to forested hills. He'd never imagined that one could travel in such comfort and style. The car's interior walls and cabinets were elaborately carved mahogany. Marble sinks, brass electric light fixtures, and richly appointed dark green velvet furnishings filled the luxurious spaces. The back of the car featured an observation deck. The parlor had three staterooms, a dining room, a bathroom, and a galley.

After seeing the disappointment on Mr. Nordeman's face, and after giving it more thought, John had decided to go to New York after all. The store could survive without him for a week. At first, Mr. Field wasn't pleased. John eventually appealed to his boss's good sense, after selling the idea that this trip would be good for research. It would be an opportunity for John to see what the best department stores in New York were doing with their display windows. The fact that Mr. Field didn't have to pay a dime of John's travel costs was a bonus.

John was enjoying this mode of travel. He would sleep in comfort tonight, and in the morning, he would be in New York City. It was a marvel.

"I wish you could come to Port Chester with me," Elizabeth said. "But still, this is nice. I'm so happy that you're here right now."

"I am too." John smiled. "So, tell me, what do I need to know before I visit the offices of Nordeman Insurance?"

"Well first, you should know there's a lot of mingling and meeting new people." For the next hour, Elizabeth went into great detail about the business and the people who worked for her father. She spoke with the vocabulary of someone well-versed and knowledgeable in business matters. John was impressed.

The next morning, after an early breakfast of bacon, eggs, and hotcakes, the train arrived at Grand Central Terminal. Elizabeth left with Sissy, her maid, to catch another train to Port Chester. She was excited to meet Catherine's new baby, a girl named Celine.

Mrs. Nordeman and John waited together on Forty-Second Street while a porter loaded their luggage onto the back of a landau that had been waiting for them when they arrived.

"This is home," Mrs. Nordeman said with a satisfied smile. John looked around and nodded with appreciation. New York was an impressive city. "Do you want to get settled into your room first? Or should we drop you off at the office along the way?"

"Well, since I had such a good night's sleep, I might as well go straight to the office. Thank you." John wanted to make a good impression on Mrs. Nordeman, and he didn't want to seem as if he was simply tagging along on the trip for leisure.

***

The last few days were far from leisurely. When John arrived at the Nordeman Insurance office, he was put to work straight away. Mr. Gates, the manager assigned to show John the office, didn't hide his displeasure at having John around. The tasks he assigned to John seemed designed to highlight John's incompetence—while at the same time, felt an awful lot like useless "busy-work." The tour of all three floors of offices never happened. Mr. Gates had escorted John to a small, windowless room, not much bigger than a closet, and left him alone.

"Stay here," Mr. Gates said. "I'll return with some paperwork I need you to do."

John hadn't realized he'd be filing stacks of paperwork and reading contracts the entire time he was in New York. Was this a test? Was Mr. Banks reporting back to Mr. Nordeman?

It didn't seem like Mr. Nordeman was the type of man to do something like that, but John did as he was told. He didn't complain, even though the work was tedious and mind-numbingly dull. It almost seemed like the other workers at the office were unaware of who he was or why he was there.

There wasn't enough time to see the city—though he'd managed to walk by the windows at B. Altman & Company. John appreciated what he saw in the displays. Disappointedly, it was already closed for the evening when he'd arrived. John would have liked to have spent more time exploring the beautiful store.

Elizabeth was returning from Port Chester on Friday afternoon, and she would be meeting her mother and John at The Plaza Hotel for dinner that night. John couldn't wait to see her again. Her mother had been busy all week too—so much so, that John had hardly seen her, even though their rooms were adjacent.

In addition to meeting up with old friends, Mrs. Nordeman had been finalizing details on their newly built house and shopping for furniture with her designer. John couldn't help thinking he was slightly jealous of her designer. What he wouldn't give to decorate the interior of that home. It sounded far more interesting than sitting at a desk in the insurance office.

Mrs. Nordeman had pointed out the mansion as their carriage drove past it on Fifth Avenue, the second day they were in the city. The stunning exterior was nearly complete. The grand American Renaissance-style structure built of white stone gleamed in the sunlight.

By late afternoon on Friday, the last day of work at Nordeman Insurance—for now—John was watching the clock on the wall, anxiously waiting until the appropriate time to leave. He would be grateful to get back to work at Marshall Field's when he returned to Chicago.

John was isolated from the other employees throughout the week, but he'd overheard snippets of hushed conversations, and he'd noticed the furtive glances cast his way whenever he approached. John was starting to see that all was not right at Nordeman Insurance. He suspected that Mr. Gates purposely kept him away from the others. What if John wasn't being tested by Mr. Nordeman, but more accurately, Mr. Gates was hiding something?

John had a suspicion that the manager didn't want him to go back to Chicago and tell Mr. Nordeman what was going on at the company. The question now was how sure was he of these suspicions? And should he voice his concerns to Mr. Nordeman?

CHAPTER TWENTY

Sissy helped Elizabeth step into the red velvet gown she'd chosen to wear to dinner that night. Turning toward the mirror in the hotel suite, Elizabeth ran a critical eye over her reflection as she waited for Sissy to fasten the long row of tiny buttons that ran up the back of her dress. Elizabeth had missed John over the last few days, and when he saw her again, she wanted to look her best. *I need to do something different with my hair.*

"Sissy, I've decided I'd like to have bangs... something similar to what Catherine has. Could you please cut some for me?"

"Now?" Sissy met Elizbeth's gaze in the mirror. She seemed uncomfortable.

"Yes, you can do it. It's just a little fringe."

Sissy didn't appear wholly convinced, but she moved toward one of the trunks and opened a drawer, pulling out the scissors. "Are you sure, miss?"

"Absolutely." Elizabeth gave Sissy what she hoped was a reassuring smile, then she sat down at the vanity and began pulling pins loose from her hair.

A few minutes, and a few snips later, Sissy put the scissors back down and gave a deep exhale, in what Elizabeth hoped, was a positive sign. During the cut, she'd faced away from the mirror.

Elizabeth turned and assessed the new hairstyle. "I love it!"

"I'm so glad, miss. I think it looks very fashionable. Now, you need some ear drops." She held up two pairs. "Rubies or pearls?"

"Pearls. And Sissy, I know you want to see your family. Please, take the rest of the evening off. I'll be fine."

Sissy smiled appreciatively. "Thank you, Miss Nordeman."

After putting on her ear drops, Elizabeth picked up her shawl and her reticule and left the room. Her mother and John would be waiting in the lobby.

The chandeliers overhead sparkled against the cream-colored walls and marble floors. Elizabeth walked past gorgeous white orchids, breathing in their tantalizing smell. Then she saw John. He looked handsome in his dinner jacket and black tie. He stood, smiled, and moved toward her. "Elizabeth, my love, it's wonderful to see you. You're beautiful. Did you do something different with your hair?"

Mrs. Nordeman, who had come down the stairs behind Elizabeth, walked over to the couple and greeted them.

"You've got bangs!" her mother said.

"Ah, that's it," John said. "I like the change."

"Yes, the look suits you," Her mother said warmly. "Well, shall we go in?" Elizabeth and John followed her into the dining room. The space was tastefully elegant, and a string quintet was playing. The tall waiter showed the group to their table and left them with menus.

"How are the Davenports?" Mother asked.

"Wonderful. Catherine loved the layette set you sent for baby Celine."

"Good, and the baby is well?"

"Oh, yes, she's quite charming. Her parents are smitten." Elizabeth was in love with the little one, as well. She was looking forward to moving back to New York so she could see her more often. Babies grew too quickly.

"And John, tell us, how was your week?" Elizabeth's mother asked, draping a napkin across her lap.

John seemed to be thinking carefully about his answer before speaking. "I'm very appreciative of the opportunity you've afforded me to come along with you and Elizabeth this week. New York is an exciting city," he said.

It didn't escape Elizabeth's notice that John had avoided directly answering the question. He said nothing about his time at Nordeman Insurance.

The waiter came to take their orders. When he left, Elizabeth's mother began explaining how the construction of the house was coming along. Elizabeth continued to pay special attention to John throughout the meal. His smile seemed forced, and he was evasive about what he'd been doing the past week.

By the time the waiter brought the cheese course, she felt sure that he was unhappy. She wanted to speak to him privately, so she was somewhat relieved when the meal was over, and her mother excused herself.

"I'm going to retire for the evening in my room. You two are welcome to linger here at the table until you're finished. We have an early train to catch. Be in the lobby, tomorrow morning, by six," her mother said.

When she was gone, Elizabeth reached across the table and touched John's hand. "I missed you."

John took her hand in his own and smiled. "I missed you too."

"How was it at the office?" Elizabeth took a sip of wine.

"It was busy, so I was probably underfoot. It will take a while to find my place there." John avoided her in the eyes when he spoke.

She decided not to pry anymore. What he expressed was probably true—he just needed time to adjust.

***

Opening day had arrived for the Columbian Exposition—May 1, 1893—and the newspapers called it "Chicago's Days of Days."

Outside, it didn't look very promising. A foggy haze covered everything. Only yesterday, it had snowed. Elizabeth couldn't see the street below from her window on the twenty-third floor. She'd woken early. Her father wanted his family to ride in the procession with him and the other dignitaries of the fair.

They would start at the Auditorium Building on Michigan Avenue, where the Duke and Duchess of Veragua were staying. The duke was a direct descendant of Christopher Columbus and an honored guest. They would stop at the Lexington Hotel, where President Cleveland would join them. The procession would finish at the Administration Building at Jackson Park, where President Grover Cleveland would officially open the fair.

Today was the day Elizabeth's father, along with countless others, had been working like mad to make a reality. It wasn't only a matter of pride for the city of Chicago, but the whole country. Elizabeth watched the ominous dark clouds. Every business in the city had closed to celebrate this day. *Please, God, send sunshine.* It was a prayer Elizabeth was certain she wasn't alone in saying that morning.

By the time Elizabeth and her parents went downstairs, a spot of blue had appeared in the sky. Crowds of people, dressed in their finest clothes, were already milling about. Outside on the street, it looked like a party—one the whole city was taking part in.

When the carriage arrived at the Auditorium Building, the spot of blue in the sky had expanded. The excitement among the crowd continued to build. Elizabeth and her family stayed in the carriage. They were now lined up behind the others that would be in the parade. She waved at Mrs. Palmer, who was directly in front of them. And then it began—the slow procession through the streets.

Elizabeth smiled and waved, enjoying a day she'd wouldn't soon forget. The buildings were adorned with festive bunting and flags. People threw confetti from high-up windows onto the street, and a brass marching band was playing.

Her father appeared happy and proud, and Elizabeth thought about how glad she was that her family had moved to Chicago for the year so he could be a part of making this day happen. *My parents are happier now, and if we wouldn't have come here, I would never have met John.* That thought reminded her to search for him in the crowd. He'd told her he would be waving and cheering them on as they went by. She had no idea how many thousands of people would be lining the streets. It was doubtful she'd spot him, but she looked anyway.

By the time they reached Jackson Park, Elizabeth was starting to feel slightly overwhelmed. She followed her family as they got out of the landau and walked toward the Administration Building where President Cleveland, and many other dignitaries, would be giving speeches. When she entered the area called the Court of Honor, she gasped. They were surrounded by gleaming buildings—palaces. The White City. Elizabeth was in awe of its magnificence. A great circular basin of water was at the center of it all, with a fountain and statues. If only John could have been with her to share this moment.

The speeches began, but Elizabeth couldn't hear what they were saying, so she let her mind wander. She wanted to get a closer view at what people were calling the Barge of State, which was in the middle of the Grand Basin. It was only a few steps away, but the crowd was dense. She moved away from her family. It was hard to navigate through the group, and before she knew it, she'd gotten lost in a sea of people.

Elizabeth, who wasn't very tall, couldn't see around her to get back to where she was supposed to be. People pressed in at every turn, blocking her view and making it impossible to get her bearings. She felt herself being swept away with the crowd. That feeling of being overwhelmed, which she'd experienced earlier, returned with a vengeance.

Her heart beat faster. Elizabeth felt numb and short of breath. The panic grew until she felt strangely detached from everything that was happening around her. Now, all she wanted was to get out of there. There were too many people. Just when she felt like she was going to fall from dizziness, she felt a firm and reassuring hand grip her elbow.

"Elizabeth, I'm here. It's okay," John said.

Elizabeth looked up. John held her gaze—the expression on his face showed compassion and

strength that calmed her. *How did he find me?*
"You're here," was all she could say.

He led her toward where her parents were
still standing. They were watching the speakers
on the stage, unaware of what had just happened
to their daughter.

Elizabeth felt better now and also a little
foolish. "Thank you," she said to John. "I'm glad
you found me."

He smiled at her and squeezed her hand. "I
am too."

The rest of the day was fun. John stayed with
Elizabeth and her parents, and the four of them
strolled around the fairgrounds. They visited the
Women's Building, which was Mrs. Palmer's pet
project, and they strolled through the Midway
Plaisance. Sadly, Mr. Ferris's Great Wheel wasn't
yet ready.

"We'll have to come back and ride the wheel
together when it opens," John said.

It was even taller than Elizabeth could have
imagined. The towers the wheel would rest on
when it was completed, dwarfed everything
around them.

"Yes, I hope we'll come back many times,"
Elizabeth said with a grin.

By the end of the day, Elizabeth realized she
must have walked many miles. Her feet were

feeling it. She was tired but happy. John rode back in the landau with the Nordeman's to the Palmer House. Neither one of them spoke of that brief but frightening moment of panic Elizabeth had experienced during the speeches. It would stay between the two of them.

Today, Elizabeth felt as if her love for John had deepened, even more than she'd previously known was possible. He'd been there for her when she needed him most, like an angel sent from heaven. He made her feel safe and loved.

May 1, 1893, was a day that wouldn't soon be forgotten—not by the citizens of Chicago, nor Elizabeth. The city had shown the world that it was one of the greats, and the optimism displayed that day would inspire, not just the people who'd been there, but countless others who heard about it, long into the future. The exposition was just getting started, though. There was still much more to look forward to.

CHAPTER TWENTY-ONE

J ohn stood close to Elizabeth on the veranda outside the ballroom at Marshall Field's home. The cool evening breeze carried with it the scent of freshly cut grass from the gardens beyond—a welcome relief from the hot, stuffy air inside. Shades of pink, purple, and red covered the twilight sky. Elizabeth hummed along to the music, which could still be heard coming from the open doors behind them. She smiled when she turned to him. A few curls had come loose from the updo she wore, which made John wonder what it was like when it was down. He wanted to run his hands through her soft hair.

Couples strolled along the paths through the maze made from shrubs, holding hands, kissing—seemingly unaware that those on the veranda could see them. John took a sip of champagne from the glass he was holding and considered, once again, whether he should tell Elizabeth how he felt about working for her father.

Between the opening of the fair, courting Elizabeth, and becoming a member of the Union League, the number of parties and balls that he'd been invited to attend had increased to a level that hardly left room for anything else. John went to as many of them as he could, but only because they were also opportunities to see Elizabeth.

Yet, except for a few stolen moments, like the one they were enjoying now, they were rarely alone. His concerns about leaving Marshall Field's for Nordeman Insurance were growing, but he'd kept those to himself. John wanted to be honest with Elizabeth and tell her, but it never seemed the right moment to bring it up.

"Did you see that chocolate cake on the buffet table?" Elizabeth asked.

John smiled. Of course, Elizabeth had noticed the dessert. She seemed to love chocolate almost as much as she loved flowers. "Would you like me to get us some cake and bring it back here? I have something I'd like to talk to you about."

"Yes, please...something you want to talk about?" She teased, imitating her father. "I'll just wait for you on that bench over there."

When John returned with two plates of dessert, Elizabeth was seated on the bench—but she wasn't alone. She was chatting with another partygoer, a woman John recognized as a customer from the store. Elizabeth looked up and smiled as John approached.

She and the other lady, who seemed to be a stern matronly sort, stood. "Mrs. DeWitt, may I introduce you to Mr. Lewis."

The woman eyed him coolly and nodded a greeting.

"Good evening, Mrs. DeWitt. Pleased to meet you," John said. "Would you like some cake?" It would have been rude to hand a piece to Elizabeth, only—and he was holding two plates. Mrs. DeWitt looked delighted—another woman who loved chocolate.

"Oh, how kind. Thank you," Mrs. DeWitt said, accepting the plate.

The ladies quickly resumed their conversation. He stepped away, discreetly to get another piece of cake for himself. But on the way to the buffet table, he was met by Mr. and Mrs. Selfridge. John's good manners compelled him to stay when they wanted to chat. One thing led to another, and soon, John was caught up in a conversation that lasted longer than he'd intended.

John finally made his way back to the veranda to search for Elizabeth, but by this point, she was gone. *She's probably inside somewhere. Is a quiet place to talk, alone, for five minutes too much to ask?* A gentle hand touched his elbow from behind.

"There was something you wanted to talk to me about?"

John turned and saw Elizabeth.

"Ah, yes—I thought I'd lost you. I'm sorry about that. I got sidetracked." John offered her his arm. "Would you like to go back outside?" Elizabeth nodded and slipped her hand into the crook of his elbow.

Lightning bugs sparked as they walked along the path through the garden, provoking Elizabeth to laugh with delight. She spoke first. "It's quite a summer to be in Chicago, isn't it?"

"That, it is." He took a deep breath. "Would you ever consider staying here? For good?"

Elizabeth remained quiet in response to John's question, apparently thinking about what to say next. She bit the corner of her lip and stared at her feet. When she looked back up and met John's gaze, her hazel eyes were filled with sadness.

"My parents need me. They're going back to New York when the fair is over, and I have to go with them. Are you having doubts, John?"

"None regarding how I feel about you. It's my role in your father's business that has me concerned. I'm not sure I'm the right person to take on such a position." *There. He'd said it.* John watched Elizabeth's face. She didn't seem surprised by his confession.

"You'll learn. I don't think you give yourself enough credit."

John tried to give Elizabeth what he hoped was a reassuring smile. He was grateful for the confidence she had in him—however misplaced he thought it might be. John pushed aside his lingering concerns, not wanting to spoil the evening. But he had a couple of questions for Elizabeth.

"What is it that you want, Elizabeth? What would make you happy?"

She laughed as if such questions were irrelevant. "*You* make me happy, John." She hesitated, growing more serious. "And I want some peace. I want to know I've done right by my family."

John desired that for her, too, and right now, he wanted to kiss her. She was close enough that he could detect the faint scent of her gardenia perfume. But he stopped himself, knowing they'd be seen. Even now, being unchaperoned, outside on the lawn, in the evening hours, was enough to raise some disapproving eyebrows.

"And you? What is it you want? What makes you happy, John?"

"You make me happy, Elizabeth. And I want the best for you." John carefully considered his next words. "Do you know your father's as-sociate, Mr. Banks, very well?

"No, I don't believe so. I think he's a newer employee. Why?"

"He didn't seem too pleased to have me around the week I was in New York. I don't know—it seemed like there was something he didn't want me to find out. It was strange. I thought I was there to meet the employees, learn about the company, and look around."

Elizabeth seemed surprised. "And you didn't get to do those things? Hmm—that was the whole reason my father wanted you to go."

"No, I worked alone, filing papers. Maybe it was a miscommunication. I know your father has been incredibly busy with his work here. I was planning on saying something to him, but I was waiting for the right time."

"I'm glad you told me, and I'm sorry that happened. No wonder you haven't seemed very excited about the company. You need a do-over. And you do realize, you'll be Mr. Banks' boss, right? You won't have to keep him around." Eliz-abeth shivered and pulled her wrap tighter.

"You're getting cold. Come on, let's go back inside." John thought about Elizabeth's words as they made their way back to the house. She was right. He needed to take another look at Norde-man Insurance. It couldn't be that bad.

And Mr. Banks? He was definitely hiding something. There didn't seem to be any other explanation for his strange behavior.

***

John put a club sandwich on his tray and sur-veyed the employee lunchroom. Though he of-ten ate lunch at the Union League now, he still liked to pop in and have lunch here at times. Mrs. Sanders and her assistant, Miss Walsh, were sitting over by the window. They were al-ways good company, and there was an empty seat at their table.

"Hello, ladies. Mind if I join you today?"

Mrs. Sanders looked up and smiled. "Please, sit down."

Miss Walsh moved a tin of cookies closer to John. "Here, help yourself. I've meant to ask, have you heard from your brother and Mary? How are the newlyweds doing?"

"I haven't received a letter in a while, but last I heard, they seemed happy. Mary is adjusting to farm life. I'm sure it's quite a change for her. Her brother, Stuart, has been a huge help to have around, according to Horace..."

Mrs. Sanders took a peanut butter cookie. "Speaking of weddings, I wanted to tell you, Mr.

Lewis, that our wedding dress sold last week. And there have been other ladies asking if we were going to carry any more ready-to-wear bridal gowns."

"We made a good team on the last one, didn't we?" John reached into the container offered and grabbed a treat.

"Yes, we did." Mrs. Sanders paused. "Now, tell us the rumors are true. Are you courting Miss Nordeman?" Mrs. Sanders asked the question, but Miss Walsh eagerly nodded her head and leaned forward, seeming eager to hear John's answer.

"Yes, I am." John suddenly felt like he was having lunch with two nosy sisters, but he smiled good-naturedly. They were well-meaning. "Where are these rumors coming from?"

Miss Walsh raised her eyebrows as if she were surprised at such a question. "Word spreads fast around here, Mr. Lewis."

"Have you looked at rings yet? You could take her to the top of the Great Wheel and ask her to marry you there! Wouldn't that be romantic?" Mrs. Sanders was getting carried away.

John laughed and brushed away the questions, claiming he needed to get back to work. He said goodbye to the ladies and left the lunchroom.

Later on, when John was walking through the jewelry department, he stopped and checked-out at the displays. He was curious. It wouldn't hurt to look. Elizabeth deserved only the best—and John figured he should probably know what kind of cost that might entail.

He thought about Mrs. Sander's idea for a proposal as one particularly beautiful diamond ring under the glass counter caught his eye. He had to admit—her plan was good.

"May I help you, Mr. Lewis?" the clerk behind the counter asked.

John scanned the area, making sure nobody else was watching. "I'd like to take a closer look at that one, right there."

The clerk took out a key and unlocked the case, then brought the ring out for John to see. "It's stunning, isn't it? Two carats."

John admired the diamond before handing it back to the clerk. "Yes, it is. Thank you. I'm just looking. But for reference, how much would one pay for a ring like this?"

John gave the clerk a nod when he was told the price, hoping to appear neutral. He'd never spent that much on anything before in his life, but maybe it was time to be less frugal. He wanted to get this right.

Two days later, John was still thinking about the diamond. At lunchtime, he decided to walk over to his bank and make a withdrawal. As he approached the building, he saw a crowd of people on the sidewalk. None of them seemed happy. Some men were pounding on the doors, which appeared to be locked. A few policemen stood nearby, warily eyeing the crowd.

"What's happening?" John asked a man standing nearby.

"We're not sure. The sign on the door says that operations have been temporarily suspended." The man's voice held a note of barely concealed panic. "I need money *now* so I can feed my family."

No, not again. John took a deep breath. Temporarily suspended didn't mean closed. Maybe it was just a precaution. *Please, God, help us all.* John read the sign on the door, needing to see for himself—it was true.

Police officers told people to disperse. There was a hint of danger in the air, and people were angry. John turned to go back to work, feeling like he'd had the wind knocked out of him.

CHAPTER TWENTY-TWO

"I'm going to the Hull House tomorrow, Elizabeth. Do you want to come with me?" Elizabeth's mother had been volunteering at the settlement house over the past couple of months. From what Elizabeth understood, this was a place where women, like her mother, helped give back to society. It was the third time in as many weeks that the same question had been asked. Elizabeth sensed her mother had found some profound purpose in this new cause she was championing. It made Elizabeth curious as to what it was all about.

"I wish I could, Mother. But I need to go into the store and finish the flower arrangements." *A commitment is a commitment, even when I'd rather be doing something else.*

Mother and daughter were dining alone in their apartment at the Palmer House that night. Elizabeth's father had another engagement with the Exposition Corporation. They rarely saw him these days.

"Well, one of these days you should come— when you can get away from your work. I think you would find it most interesting," her mother said, buttering her roll.

"I'd like that. I don't mean to be putting you off. I really would like to visit."

The next day, when Elizabeth was in the basement studio of Marshall Field's, putting together floral arrangements, John came into the room.

"I need to talk to you about something," he said with a concerned expression on his face.

"Yes? What is it?"

"Management has requested I make some temporary cutbacks in my budget. I'm going to have to pare down our flower order to half of what it has been. The quality of your work is outstanding. It has nothing to do with that. It's just business. Shoppers have been spending less lately."

The poor guy looked like he expected her to be upset with him. She wasn't. A part of her was pleased that she'd have more free time. Maybe she could fit in a visit to Hull House with her mother next week.

"I understand, John. I'm not disappointed. It's a perfectly reasonable business decision."

John smiled. "Thank you for being so understanding." He studied the vase she'd just put together. "It's not something I wanted to do." He paused, then picked up a rose from the table, bringing it to his nose to inhale its scent. "These are beautiful."

Elizabeth nodded. "Since there will be less to do, I suppose I'll only need to come in once a week. Will that be acceptable?"

After John left, a few minutes later, Elizabeth finished up her task and turned out the lights in the studio. She liked working here, and though she'd pretended with John that she was okay with the changes, there was a part of her that was disappointed.

***

Hull House, named after its original owner, was an old mansion on the west side of Chicago. It was run by two women—Jane Addams and Ellen Gates Starr. Their purpose was to provide social and educational opportunities for working-class people in the neighborhood.

Elizabeth's mother explained the role Hull House had taken in the community as they rode along the dusty roads, away from the center of town. The buildings became shabbier, the streets, dirtier. Laundry hung from lines strung from building to building. Barefoot children wearing tattered rags played outside, shouting to each other in Italian. The stench of garbage in the hot midday sun was almost overpowering.

Elizabeth was surprised her mother had been spending so much of her time there. "What do you do when you're here?" she asked with curiosity.

"I like to help with the kindergarten class. Sometimes I hold the babies in the nursery." This was a side of her mother that Elizabeth hadn't seen before. "There's also a music school, which I thought you might be interested in." Her mother smiled and pointed toward a beautiful but old and somewhat decaying brick mansion on the right. The carriage stopped in front of it. "This is it, Hull House."

The building appeared out of place with its plain surroundings, and Elizabeth was sure she must have appeared equally so in her pink walking suit with its giant puffy sleeves. *Why didn't Mother tell me to wear something else?* She set aside that discomfort, however, after entering the house. The home was spacious and furnished tastefully—all very pleasing. Elizabeth relaxed, feeling less out of place now than she had a few minutes before out on the street. She could hear children's voices, singing from the next room.

"Hello, Mrs. Nordeman," a thin, middle-aged woman wearing spectacles said as she approached them. "You must be *Miss* Nordeman.

Your mother has told me so much about you—all good, mind you. Welcome, I'm Miss Starr."

An hour later, Elizabeth found herself sitting on a piano bench, helping a young girl named Angelina work her way through a complicated piece of sheet music by Mozart. Angelina was a sweet girl—shy but determined when it came to learning how to play the piano. Elizabeth guessed she was somewhere around the age of twelve.

"How long have you been taking lessons?" she asked the girl.

"I've been coming here for about a year now," Angelina said in a strong Italian accent.

Elizabeth nodded. The girl was quite accomplished for someone with only a year of training behind her. "You're very good. You must practice a lot."

Angelina smiled and looked down. "Thank you. Will you play something for me?"

Elizabeth played "Moonlight Sonata" by Beethoven, a piece she'd memorized.

When she finished, Angelina's eyes were shining. "That was beautiful."

"Would you like to learn how to play it?" Elizabeth asked. "Maybe the sheet music is already here. If not, I'll bring it with me next time I come."

"Oh, yes. Thank you!"

And with that, Elizabeth knew she'd be back the following week. "I'll leave you to practice now. I'll see if I can't find that piece for you to play."

Outside the practice room, in the hallway, Elizabeth searched for Miss Davy, the music instructor who'd introduced her to Angelina.

"Who are you looking for? Maybe I can help," a woman said.

Elizabeth hadn't noticed the woman until now. She sat near a potted palm in the corner with a book in hand. When she lowered the volume from in front of her, Elizabeth tried not to gasp. The woman, who was otherwise quite beautiful, had a black eye patch covering half her face.

"I was seeking Miss Davy or someone else who could direct me to where the sheet music is kept."

"Miss Davy is with another student right now, but the music is in the library. I'll show you." The woman put her book down and stood to greet Elizabeth. "I'm Mrs. Rossi, Angelina's mother. I heard you playing for Angelina. It was lovely. Thank you for helping my daughter. She loves music, and I'm no help whatsoever. I don't read music."

Elizabeth followed Mrs. Rossi to the library and was soon engaged in conversation with the woman, who was far less shy than her daughter. At first, it was hard to avoid staring at the eye-patch. Mrs. Rossi had the same lilting Italian rhythm to her speech, which Elizabeth loved listening to.

As the women searched through the files for "Moonlight Sonata," Elizabeth learned more about Angelina and her mother. They lived nearby and frequently visited Hull House together. Angelina received her piano lessons and practiced here, and Mrs. Rossi participated in sewing classes.

"We came here from Italy when Angelina was only six. Angelina's older sister, Sophia, died a year later of pneumonia. They were two years apart in age."

"I'm sorry for your loss. My brother died a couple of years ago." Elizabeth was shocked to hear herself saying those words to someone who was practically a stranger. But she felt comfortable with Mrs. Rossi.

"Let's go to the kitchen and get some tea. Then we can sit down and talk some more," Mrs. Rossi said.

Elizabeth sat down at the kitchen table and waited while Mrs. Rossi, who seemed very much at home at Hull House, put a kettle on the stove to boil. Should Elizabeth be doing something and not just sitting around, talking? But she wanted to hear more of Mrs. Rossi's story—and she sensed the woman needed someone to talk to.

"Mrs. Rossi, I have the sheet music that we couldn't find at home. I'll bring it with me next week. I would love to work with your daughter more."

"Thank you. She will love that. And please, call me Maria." She placed a teacup in front of Elizabeth. "Now, I want to hear your story. What brings you here today?"

"I came with my mother. I was curious about this place, since she seems to love it so much. We're from New York." Elizabeth began to tell Maria more of her story—her brother, the fire, moving to Chicago. Again, she surprised herself with her candor, but the woman's warmth and kindness drew her in.

Maria, Elizabeth learned, was supporting Angelina by herself. "There are good people here. Miss Addams and Miss Starr helped me out of a bad situation. My husband had his demons. I wear this eyepatch because I don't have my left eye anymore. He drank a lot, and when he did, he took his problems out on me. That's how it happened—a fist to my face. Angelina saw it happen. She ran and told the police, and later, they took him away."

Elizabeth reached across the table and put her hand on Maria's. She had no words for something so terrible.

"We didn't have money for food or rent after that. We started coming here for dinner. I want to earn an honest living, so I've been learning to sew. My husband never hurt Angelina though, and before he was gone, we'd always had enough to eat. I felt guilty that I couldn't provide for Angelina." Maria dabbed a tissue to her eye. "My own failures contributed to the situation. I should have prepared better. I figured it would eventually come to this—that I would need to provide for both of us. But our life is better now. God has taken care of us. I've let go of the guilt. I have so much to be thankful for."

Thankful? "It doesn't sound like you have anything to feel guilty about," Elizabeth said.

"But guilt is a strange thing, isn't it? We can't choose our emotions. We can only choose how we respond to them."

Isn't that the truth? Elizabeth wiped away a tear that spilled onto her cheek. "What will happen to your husband? Will they keep him locked away?" Elizabeth took another sip of tea but quickly set the teacup down. It was now cold.

"He's in heaven now."

A man like that, in heaven? Why would she say that? The shock must have shown on Elizabeth's face because Maria gave her an understanding smile.

"I know how that sounds. But in one of my lowest moments, I read a verse in Ephesians that changed everything for me. 'For it is by grace you have been saved, through faith—and this is not from yourselves, it is the gift of God—not by works, so that no one can boast.'" A shy smile came over Maria's face. "For me, once I understood that I'm saved by grace, and all I need to do is receive it like a gift, I was free to begin a new life. My husband became very sick while he was in jail. I used to visit him. I told him I forgave him for what he did to me, and I shared that verse with him. Before he died, he apologized to me, and he told me about his newfound faith in Christ. I think he's in heaven now, and he's a new man."

Elizabeth sat, stunned, and completely in awe of the woman in front of her. Maria had been through so much heartache and pain, and though Elizabeth had set out to do good for the people she met at Hull House that day, she was the one who was receiving a great gift.

Maria's words were more than mere platitudes. They were sincerely spoken truths, full of wisdom and grace. A common thread connected Elizabeth's story with Maria's, and even though they came from two very different backgrounds, they were drawn together.

Though Elizabeth rarely read her Bible, when she returned home later that afternoon, she pulled it out and searched for the verses in Ephesians that Maria had quoted. She found them in the second chapter and the eighth and ninth verses. When it was time to get dressed for dinner, she left her Bible on her nightstand, open to those pages.

CHAPTER TWENTY-THREE

The bank reopened on Monday. Customers were allowed to withdraw limited amounts of money, but John felt reassured that decision was a step in the right direction. If he wanted to buy the ring, he'd need to take out installments of cash from his savings, a little at a time, until it was all there. So, on Wednesday morning, for the third day in a row, John skipped lunch and went to the bank during his lunch hour. The line was long and slow.

"You know, I heard some of the banks have been hiring extra people to stand here and pretend to take out money, just to slow things down and discourage bank runs," the man behind John said.

John looked around. People were queued up from the front doors, all the way down the steps and out to the street corner. He'd been standing in one place for the last twenty minutes with barely a step forward. "That could be true," John replied.

With the current amount the bank was allowing customers to make on daily withdrawals, John figured these lunchtime trips would need to continue for another week. He let out a deep sigh, and his stomach let out a grumble. Tomorrow, he'd pack a lunch.

"Want a donut?" The man behind John opened a brown paper bag and held it toward him. "I'm Nick Bates." He looked like a man who probably worked at the nearby railyard. A working man who was tall, young, and friendly.

"Thank you. I'm John Lewis." John reached into the bag and took out a powdered sugar donut and nodded in gratitude as he took a bite. Upon tasting its sweetness, John's mood improved considerably. The line moved forward two more steps.

"Have you been to the fair yet?" Mr. Bates asked.

"Just once, when it opened, but I'm hoping to go back soon. How about you?"

"Not yet. I'm taking my family tomorrow. I've got two sons, three daughters, and a Mrs. at home. That's why I'm here. I've been saving up for this day for a long time."

"That's funny. It's sort of what brings me here too. I'm going to propose to my girl on top of the Great Wheel."

Mr. Bates chuckled. "Well, after all this waiting, you've had plenty of time to think carefully about your decision. I wish you all the best!"

John smiled and said goodbye. It was finally his turn to approach the teller. The wait had gone more quickly once he'd found someone to talk to.

With his errand finished, John made his way back to Marshall Field's to finish out the workday. Mr. Bates was right. John had thought carefully about his decision. He wanted to make Elizabeth his wife—and only the best ring would do. The dreary headlines announcing bank failures and a Wall Street crash had caused a brief wavering in John's resolve, but not anymore. John was sure. He only hoped the ring would still be available by the time he'd gathered the funds.

***

Cornelius Nordeman was already seated at a table in the corner when John arrived at the Union League for their arranged lunch meeting. Though the question he wanted to ask Elizabeth's father would not be unexpected, John's hands were tingling, and his throat was parched. *Water—I need water.*

As he approached the table, Elizabeth's father looked up and nodded in greeting. "Hello, Mr. Nordeman. Thank you for meeting me today," John said, choking out the words. A glass of water with ice in it was already waiting for him. He sat down and nearly knocked it over in his haste to take a drink.

After a few brief words of greeting, Mr. Nordeman returned to studying his menu. "So, John, what was it you wanted to ask me about today?" The man was direct.

John gulped. He might as well get straight to the point. "Sir, I asked you to meet me here today because I love your daughter, and I would like to ask for your blessing for us to marry."

Mr. Nordeman put down his menu and regarded John. His expression gave no hint of what he was thinking. Just then, the waiter came to take their order. "I'll have the special, and bring a bottle of claret, please."

"I'll have the special as well," John said.

The waiter left, and Mr. Nordeman slowly stirred a spoonful of sugar into his coffee. "She means the world to me," he said. "Elizabeth is an independently-minded woman, and I know she cares for you. I believe you're a good man, John, and I admire your work ethic. I give you my blessing."

"Thank you, sir." John hesitated. "There's one more thing I need to ask. I need your help getting Elizabeth to Ferris's Wheel."

***

It was a clear morning when John and the Nordemans set out for the fair. The ring was in John's front jacket pocket, and he stopped himself from reaching for it again. If he weren't careful, it would become obvious that he was hiding something.

At 9:00 a.m., the sun was already beating down on them in the open carriage. Elizabeth opened her lace parasol and smiled at John. "I'm so happy you and Father took the day off work so we could do this together. I'm even more excited about the fair this time, now that I know something of what to expect!" Her eyes sparkled as she spoke.

They entered the fairgrounds through the Cottage Grove Avenue entrance to the Midway. After walking through the Bedouin Encampment, Mr. Nordeman looked at John, gave a wink, and announced that he was going to take his wife on the Captive Balloon. "We'll catch up with you two later. How about we meet for lunch in Old Vienna at one?"

John and Elizabeth wandered through the Ostrich Farm for a while after that. "Let's go on the Great Wheel." Elizabeth pointed toward the massive structure, not far away, which dwarfed everything around it.

"Now?" John was almost sure he could hear his heart thumping in his chest. "All right."

Hundreds of people were queued up. They stretched from the entrance, up a long set of stairs, to the loading platform. Even though the wheel could accommodate over two thousand passengers at a time, there was still a significant number of people waiting for their turn to get into the cars. After multiple days of spending his lunch hour in the bank line, preparing for this moment, John found some humor in this final arrangement. *What was one more line?*

A brass band played nearby. John enjoyed seeing Elizabeth's excitement as they moved closer toward the platform. The wheel was majestic as it slowly revolved in its circle. Together, they watched and listened as people who were exiting the ride walked by, exclaiming about the wonders they'd seen. But as they got closer, Elizabeth's expression began to change from one of happy anticipation to fear. She frowned as she peered upward toward the top of the wheel. At this point, they'd been in line for thirty minutes.

"Are you okay?" John hoped she wasn't having second thoughts about going on the ride.

"Yes, I'm fine—I think. It sure is high. Have there been any accidents on this contraption?"

"No, not that I know of." John took Elizabeth's hand and held it.

"I don't think I can do it. I'm sorry. I can't." Elizabeth scanned the area, as if searching for a way out.

John tried to hide his disappointment. "That's all right. We can leave—but are you sure?"

Elizabeth took a deep breath and closed her eyes for a moment. After she exhaled, she straightened her shoulders. John watched as she bit her lower lip—something she often did when she was thinking. He didn't want to push her, so he waited quietly for her answer. spoke.

"Okay," she finally said. "I'm going to do it. But I don't know if I'll be able to look out the windows—"

"One step at a time." John smiled. He wasn't surprised at the turnaround. Elizabeth was the kind of woman who could push through her fears.

For the next ten minutes, John did his best to distract Elizabeth from her worries. He bought them some caramel and molasses covered popcorn mixed with peanuts from a cart nearby. It was called Cracker Jack. By the time they'd finished the snack, they'd advanced to the loading platform, and it was time to get on.

They handed over their tickets to a conductor and entered the carriage. There was room inside for about forty people. It wasn't very private. Five broad plate-glass windows were inserted on each side of the car, and swivel chairs were screwed to the floor.

The conductor closed the door, and Elizabeth reached for John's hand. He knew she was still nervous. The conductor began explaining what to expect. "The car will stop six times during the first revolution as the other carriages are emptied and refilled. Then we will revolve once without stopping. The entire ride will take around forty minutes."

They started to ascend, and as they went higher, the view outside expanded. The fairgrounds and the city lay below, and there was a clear view of Lake Michigan. When they reached the top, the conductor pointed out Michigan, Wisconsin, and Indiana. The scene was spectacular.

Elizabeth began to relax. John was happy to see that she seemed to be enjoying herself. "John, it's so beautiful—"

The outside landscape was stunning, but the woman right in front of John enchanted him even more. The wheel stopped. Was this the right time to ask?

John reached into his front jacket pocket and pulled out the ring. He kneeled on one knee in front of Elizabeth and held it out to her. "Elizabeth, I love you. Will you marry me?"

"Yes!" Elizabeth was grinning. She gasped when she looked more closely at the ring, which was exactly the reaction John had been hoping for. "I love you too," she whispered in his ear.

He slipped the ring on her finger, and it fit perfectly. The people around them were watching now, and they began clapping and hollering. John had imagined this moment for so long. It was more wonderful than anything he'd dreamed of. "You've made me so happy."

"You're such a romantic, John, and you make me happy too." She paused. "Were my parents in on this?"

John laughed. "Yes, so it would have been pretty awkward if you'd said no."

"How could I say no to you?" Elizabeth kissed him on the cheek, then with her lips close to his ear, she whispered, "The only complaint I have about this moment is that everyone is watching us—and I'd like to kiss you properly."

CHAPTER TWENTY-FOUR

The grand opening of Marshall Field's new annex was only three weeks away. Elizabeth was counting down the days. Though the expansion was exciting, and she was proud of John's contributions to the beautiful new space, the primary reason behind her enthusiasm boiled down to the fact that she missed her fiancé.

Until the big day, John would be fully occupied with preparations at the store. After the opening, John would give his notice of resignation to Mr. Field's, and they could begin planning the next phase of their life together.

It wouldn't be time to get ready for dinner for another hour yet, so Elizabeth wandered into the library to choose a book. It was too hot to do much of anything else. There, she found her mother, quietly reading. "The air is stifling in this apartment, isn't it?"

"Have some sweet iced tea, dear, and sit down." Her mother rang a bell, calling for Annette to bring another glass. "Your father will be working late tonight. It will be just the two of us for dinner."

Elizabeth's father had been working late most nights. Contrary to what she thought would be a lightening of his responsibilities once the fair opened, they'd only multiplied. "I guess we're both looking forward to fall. The fair will be over, the annex at Marshall Field's will be open..."

Mother smiled. "Yes, that is true. In the meantime, why don't you come to New York with me for a few days? The house should be just about finished. I want to oversee a few last details, so it will be ready when we go back for good."

Some travel would help the time pass more quickly. "When are you leaving?"

"The day after tomorrow."

"I'd like that. Perhaps we can meet with a dressmaker while we're there," Elizabeth said.

Annette brought in the glass of tea, and Mother resumed reading. Elizabeth opened the newspaper and scanned the headlines. Another bank failure and panic on Wall St.—not a fine time for business owners.

Her father has been preoccupied with the Columbian Exposition, and it had never seemed like the right time to bring it up, but now, Elizabeth's thoughts returned to the conversation she'd had with John regarding Mr. Banks, her father's associate.

Maybe I'll make a surprise visit to the office while I'm there—just to check on things.

***

Elizabeth tipped the bellhop and surveyed her suite at The Plaza. The view from the windows, which looked out onto Central Park, was framed by gray velvet drapes that matched the rest of the furnishings. It was an elegant room—large and comfortable. It was good to be back in New York.

Ignoring her luggage, for now, Elizabeth walked over to a round table in the center of the sitting room. The hotel had left welcome gifts— an arrangement of pink and white roses and a box of chocolates. She'd just popped a caramel-filled chocolate into her mouth when her mother came into the room.

"We may as well head over to the house now. Are you ready to go?" her mother asked.

Elizabeth was excited to see what kind of progress had been made on the house, but she didn't feel like her mind would be at rest until she'd personally looked in at Nordeman Insurance. "I thought I'd go into the office today, instead, and see if there's anything I can do or any messages I can take back for Father."

"It's really not necessary, dear. Your father has it all under control." Her mother had never shown an interest in the business, and she wasn't keen on her daughter getting involved, either.

Nordeman Insurance could wait, Elizabeth supposed. What was one more day? "All right, I'll come with you to the house today, but I'd like to go into the office tomorrow."

Elizabeth grabbed her parasol, her gloves, and her reticule and followed her mother out of the room. They would walk, as their home was only a short distance up Fifth Avenue.

As they approached the house, it was strangely quiet. It was apparent there were no workers on the site. The construction seemed to be at a standstill. Elizabeth's mother frowned. "Where is everyone?"

"Maybe they're inside," Elizabeth said, marching up the steps to the entrance.

The front door was locked, so Mother took out her key. When they entered, they were surprised to see that the interior was still unfinished, and nobody was there. "This doesn't seem right. Let's go downtown. I want to visit Mr. Olson's office and see what this is all about. He's our contractor, so he should know."

After the walk back to The Plaza and a short wait for a carriage, Elizabeth and her mother headed out on a new mission. Neither one of them spoke as they rode along West Fifty-Seventh Street. Tension filled the air. Mrs. Nordeman was clearly unhappy with the current state of her home. Elizabeth didn't envy Mr. Olson. Her mother could be formidable when the need arose.

The coachman parked in front of a modest corner market. "What are we doing here?" Elizabeth asked her mother.

"Mr. Olson's office is on the second floor, above the market." Her mother led the way up a staircase and down a long hallway until they came to a frosted glass door. Mrs. Nordeman walked right in.

They entered a small stuffy room where a portly middle-aged man sat behind a desk, reading. Elizabeth assumed this must be Mr. Olson.

When he looked up, he didn't seem the least bit surprised to see his visitors. "Mrs. Nordeman. How do you do?"

Elizabeth's mother got straight to her point. "Mr. Olson, this is my daughter, Elizabeth Nordeman. We just came from the job site. Why isn't any work being done on my home?"

Mr. Olson cleared his throat. "They're working on another project right now, ma'am—until we can get the financial obligations squared away. I need to be able to pay my men."

"What do you mean, sir, about financial obligations? Hasn't my husband's representative paid you?"

"No, ma'am. I've sent several letters, but I haven't received a response. I'm sure it's some kind of mix-up, but in the meantime—I'm glad you're here. As soon as I'm paid, I'll send my men back out on the job."

Elizabeth's mother looked horrified, but she kept her tone calm. "Yes, I'm sure it's just a mix-up. I apologize for the delay in payment. I'll get to the bottom of this. I wasn't aware. I'll be back with your money. Good day, sir."

Elizabeth, who hadn't said a word the entire time, merely nodded farewell toward Mr. Olson and followed her mother out of the office. Mother strode back to the carriage, seemingly anxious to get out of there. "I'm sure there's a reasonable explanation, Mother. We'll figure it out." Elizabeth tried to calm her mother.

"Yes, yes—you're right. I'll send a telegram to your father as soon as we get back to the hotel. I just hope the project hasn't been put too far behind. I'd hoped to start moving furniture into the house this week. Now, it appears *that* won't be happening." Her mother sighed.

They returned to The Plaza, and Elizabeth offered to take care of sending a telegram to her father. It gave her a convenient excuse to leave their rooms again. While she was out, she also intended to make a surprise visit to Nordeman Insurance. Elizabeth said nothing about her growing sense of dread to her mother. There was no point in upsetting her further—not until she knew more. But something was definitely wrong.

Wasn't Mr. Banks the person responsible for making those missed payments? Elizabeth reminded herself not to let her suspicions get carried away from her. The facts would come to light. She found the concierge in the lobby and asked for another carriage. While she waited, she stopped by the front desk and sent a telegram to Chicago.

A young woman Elizabeth didn't recognize sat at the front desk in the lobby of her father's office when she arrived. "May I help you, miss?"

"I'm Miss Nordeman, and I'm here to see Mr. Banks."

"He isn't here right now."

"Do you know when he'll be back?"

"I don't. We haven't seen him here in a week." The corners of the secretary's mouth turned up, smugly, when she said this—as if it brought her some satisfaction to relay this bit of news to the boss's daughter.

"Please show me to his office, Miss..."

"Miss Adams. I'm not sure I should."

"Am I correct that Mr. Banks has the accounting books in his office? I need to see them."

Miss Adams still seemed unsure, but she complied and showed Elizabeth the way. The building seemed unusually quiet. The secretary looked like she was going to change her mind when she hesitated outside the door. "Miss Nordeman, we haven't been paid in more than a month. Some of the employees have already left. What's going on?"

"I don't know. But I can assure you, we'll make it right. I'm so sorry."

Once she was inside Mr. Banks' office, Elizabeth began searching through the desk drawers. She wasn't sure what she was searching for—except answers. The accounting books were in a cabinet nearby and so were several large stacks of unpaid invoices. The ledgers appeared orderly. Elizabeth spotted several recent entries showing payments had gone out to Mr. Olson's contracting business. Somebody was lying. She scooped up the books and left the office.

If Mr. Banks suddenly appeared, Elizabeth didn't want to be around—and she didn't want these books, if they contained evidence of wrongdoing, left behind, only to disappear. *I'll take these back to the hotel for safekeeping.*

On the way out, Elizabeth thanked Miss Adams and promised that she'd be in touch soon. "If Mr. Banks returns, please call The Plaza and leave a message for me. I want to know right away."

When she got back to the hotel, Elizabeth stopped by the front desk to see if her father had responded to her telegram. She breathed a sigh of relief when the clerk handed her a piece of paper that said Western Union across the top. He was on his way to New York. He was taking the overnight train and would be there by to-morrow night.

***

The next few days were a continuous unfolding of an awful series of revelations—every one more terrible than the last. Mr. Banks, who was now missing, had been stealing from Nordeman Insurance and also from the family's personal accounts. The depth of deception and the amount of money that was missing was astounding.

Elizabeth's father looked like he'd aged another twenty years overnight. He didn't want to leave his rooms at The Plaza, so the family ordered room service and shared their meals together in private.

"I'm going to sell the cottage in Newport," Father announced one night over dinner.

Mother gasped. "Is that really necessary?"

"Dear, I'm not going to mince words here. It's bad. I don't even know if I'm going to be able to save the company."

Elizabeth was saddened by the thought of her family losing the house in Newport, and she was horrified at the idea of Nordeman Insurance not making it through this crisis.

But then she thought of the women she'd met at Hull House, and she realized this was not a time to be feeling sorry for herself. People would lose their jobs if the company went under. Elizabeth understood her father already felt heartbroken, so she forced a smile onto her face. "We'll get through this. Whatever it takes. We've been through worse."

Her father smiled and kissed the top of his daughter's head as he stood to get up from the table. "You're right, Elizabeth. But please, say a prayer for us tonight."

CHAPTER TWENTY-FIVE

"There's nothing like it." Elizabeth looked around at the opulent store. "It's beautiful. You've done well."

Though John had been hearing variations of these words spoken to him throughout the evening, they sounded the sweetest coming from Elizabeth. A well-dressed crowd of Chicago's finest citizens mingled about on the first floor of the luxurious new annex at Marshall Field's for a private party celebrating tomorrow's grand opening.

John took two glasses of champagne from a silver tray as a waiter passed by and handed one to his bride-to-be. "I've heard quite a few compliments about the flowers tonight. You have an important part in all of this too."

Elizabeth and her mother had returned from New York the week before. Her father had stayed behind. John had been so busy preparing for the opening, he'd barely had time to sit down with Elizabeth and talk. She'd told him enough, though. The Nordeman's were facing a crisis.

"My mother is ready to leave, and I am too. Why don't you stop by the Palmer House after you're done here? We need to talk." Elizabeth looked as lovely as ever, but she had dark circles under her eyes. She was exhausted.

After another hour of greeting customers and friends, John was able to slip out of the party and walk the short distance down State Street. He greeted Mr. Harris, the now-familiar doorman, when he entered the Palmer House Hotel. Upstairs, Annette showed John into the Nordeman's sitting room where Elizabeth was waiting for him.

Elizabeth glanced up and smiled.

At least she's still smiling.

"Would you like some tea? My mother has already gone to bed."

"Yes, thank you." It felt awkward to bring up all that had happened in the last few weeks. One crucial question had loomed in the back of John's mind. Before, the understanding had been that he'd give his notice at Marshall Field's as soon as the annex opened. But now? He wasn't so sure.

"I have a lot to tell you," Elizabeth began. "Nordeman Insurance is in trouble. My father has an offer from another insurance company to take over the business, along with the debt. All the employees will keep their jobs. It's the only way he'll have it."

John nodded. He was thankful he hadn't given his notice to Marshall Field yet. "So, what's next?"

"A condition of this deal is that he has to sign a non-compete agreement. He can't start a new business anywhere east of the Mississippi. So, he wants to sell everything and use the proceeds to start fresh in Seattle."

"Seattle? Wow—"

"I know. I've never been there. My father has some connections. He says it's a beautiful city, and it's growing quickly. You still have a place in the company, of course. He'll get it up and running, then turn it over to you." Elizabeth anxiously steeled herself for what was next. "So, what do you say?"

John wasn't sure what to think. He wasn't expecting this. "I believe you should run the business. You're better equipped than I am. I'm just a humble window dresser."

"You underestimate yourself." Elizabeth laughed. She seemed to think he was joking. He wasn't.

"When does this all happen?"

"After the house in New York sells, and after the fair is over."

"And what do you think about moving to Seattle?"

"I agree with my father. I believe it sounds like a great place to start fresh. I don't want my parents to go out there by themselves. It's so far, and they're getting older. They need us."

"We still haven't set a date for the wedding."

"Yes, there's still a lot we need to discuss, but I'm getting tired, and I know you have an early morning tomorrow at the store. Do you want to come here for dinner after work?"

John agreed. He kissed Elizabeth as he said goodbye. On his walk home, John thought about what it would mean to move to Seattle and work for Mr. Nordeman. Starting a new company was even more daunting than taking over an already established one.

As he passed by Marshall Field's on the way home, he checked out the window displays. John allowed himself to feel a small bit of pride. His hard work had paid off. The store looked fantastic, and tonight's party was only a preview of what was ahead tomorrow. He couldn't wait to see the customer's faces in the morning when the doors of the annex were opened to the public.

***

"The house in New York sold yesterday. We didn't expect it to happen so fast."

John nodded and watched as Elizabeth stuck a sprig of Ammi Majus into a vase full of yellow chrysanthemums. "Does that mean we need to move up the wedding?"

"Yes," Elizabeth said. She hoped this was good news to John, and she anxiously searched his face for his reaction.

They were alone in the new floral studio. The tall windows provided ample light, and the new space was a welcome change from the former dark basement room. During the construction of the annex, John had always thought of this room as Elizabeth's. He was sad to realize that she would only get to enjoy it for a short while.

The grand opening was held two days ago, but John still hadn't said a word to his boss about his plans. The other night, he and Elizabeth had settled on a New York wedding in the spring, followed by a move to Washington state. John would then begin working with Mr. Nordeman to establish the new company in Seattle. Now that the fair was over, there wasn't anything holding the Nordeman family to Chicago. And now, they didn't have anything holding them to New York, either.

It was too much. Moving across the country, quitting a job he was good at—and enjoyed—taking on a position he knew he wasn't qualified for in a company that didn't even exist yet. John kept asking himself, *why?*

The hesitancy John had been feeling crystallized into something he could grab hold of. "I don't want to run an insurance company, Elizabeth. I like the job I have."

Silence filled the space between them for an agonizingly long time.

"So, what you're saying is—now that the job is no longer attached to a fortune, you don't want it?" she asked, breaking the quiet, but with ice in her tone. "You don't want me?"

She had it all wrong. *Of course, I want you.* "I love you, Elizabeth. That's not true! It was never about a fortune. I can see how you might think this looks. I should have spoken up a long time ago."

"Yes, you should have. I was clear from the start. I can't let my family down." Elizabeth's tone was curt.

Elizabeth wasn't hearing him right. He'd messed up. John meant what he'd said, but she'd misunderstood.

John watched in despair as the woman he adored stormed out of the room. He put his head on the table, wishing he could start the conversation all over again and explain what he meant.

Then Elizabeth came back. For a split second, John felt some hope. But then, she handed him her ring.

"You can have this back," she said.

John sat in stunned silence. Before he'd fully realized what had happened, she was gone.

CHAPTER TWENTY-SIX

Elizabeth gave a small wave from the back row of chairs in the parlor at Hull House and smiled when she caught Angelina's glance. Angelina seemed to be looking for her. Today, the young pianist would be performing "Moonlight Sonata," the piece Elizabeth had been helping her with. Angelina, who was sitting in the front row with the other students, was wearing a new white dress and a matching satin bow in her dark hair. She looked pretty and poised.

A bittersweet feeling settled over Elizabeth as she listened to the other piano students play. The fondness she'd developed for these children over the past couple of months made it hard to say goodbye, but Elizabeth reminded herself that today was a celebration. The hard work, the love, and the long hours of practice these kids poured into their music showed. Their pride was evident as they finished their performances and basked in the warmth of the audience's applause.

Elizabeth was seated next to her mother. In less than a week, they would be on their way to

Washington State to start a new life. Their personal belongings in the apartment at the Palmer House were now packed for the most part. Her father wanted to get his business up and running before the end of the year. Her parents were both confused and saddened over the breakup between her and John, but Elizabeth didn't want them to worry. She did her best to put on a brave face and explained as little as possible.

When it was Angelina's turn to approach the piano, Elizabeth knew that her student was nervous. Earlier, Angelina told her how scared she was to play in front of people, but nobody would guess by looking at the girl. She was as composed as any experienced performer, and when she began playing, she did so with skill—but it was the emotion she played with that was profoundly moving.

Elizabeth could tell the music came from her heart. Angelina had experienced more heartache than any young girl should have to endure in her short twelve years. She used those experiences to draw from when playing her music. It was something that couldn't be taught, and it was what set the girl apart as a gifted artist. Angelina's life, much like her mother's, was an example of grace and resilience. Both the girl and her mother inspired Elizabeth.

By the time Angelina had finished playing "Moonlight Sonata," many in the audience, including Elizabeth, were dabbing tissues at the corners of their eyes. When Angelina stood and curtsied, confidence shone through with her sweet smile.

The recital concluded, and everyone gathered in the dining room for cookies and coffee. Elizabeth said goodbye to Maria. She told her that today would be the last time she would be visiting Hull House before leaving for Seattle. When Maria wrapped her in a hug, it was hard to keep her emotions in check. Goodbyes were awful.

Elizabeth needed to talk to Angelina. A crowd of people had gathered around the girl, with everyone wanting to congratulate her on her performance. When the excitement settled down somewhat, Elizabeth took Angelina aside. "I'm moving to Seattle next week with my family. I'm going to miss you."

"You are? Will you write to me? I'm going to miss you." Angelina paused. "When are you getting married?"

"That's something else I was going to tell you. There isn't going to be a wedding anymore. It's for the best, so don't worry. And yes, of course, I'll write to you."

Angelina bit her bottom lip. "I hope so. You look sad—I'm sorry."

Elizabeth pulled up the corners of her mouth into a smile. "I'm all right. I promise." She tried to change the subject. "You played beautifully today. I can't help but imagine that you'll do great things with that talent of yours."

"Thank you, Miss Nordeman. But why aren't you getting married anymore?"

"We wanted different things in life. That's all." Did that sound convincing to Angelina?

The girl's inquiries were making Elizabeth uncomfortable. Ordinarily, she'd have put any person who asked such personal questions in their place, promptly shutting them down. But Angelina didn't know any better, and she was only curious because she cared.

Elizabeth didn't even believe the words that were coming out of her mouth. *Different things?* But what was she supposed to say? She'd ruined something wonderful, and she was sorry for it. But now wasn't the time to think about such things. A part of her felt she deserved this unhappiness. It was like a black cloud that threatened to swallow her whole. *Maybe this is my penance.*

Her mother, accompanied by Maria, joined them just then. Elizabeth was relieved, hoping this meant the interrogation was finished. "Elizabeth, are you ready to go?" Mother asked.

"Yes." Elizabeth gathered her new friends close. "You two take care. And keep practicing, Angelina."

Maria handed Elizabeth a card with their address on it. "Make sure you write. We'll be looking forward to hearing all about Seattle."

Angelina hugged Elizabeth. "Wanting different things doesn't mean you can't still get married and be happy—not if you love each other. Everyone deserves love."

Later, when Elizabeth was alone with her mother in the carriage on the way home, she leaned back against the seat and closed her eyes. She was exhausted.

"What was Angelina talking about back there?" her mother asked.

Elizabeth didn't want to discuss it anymore. "I don't know. The girl is a hopeless romantic, that's all."

"Well, she's wise beyond her years, is what I think."

Elizabeth closed her eyes again and pretended to sleep. She was surprised her mother agreed with Angelina. But then again, neither one of them were aware of the whole story. She'd been rash in her judgment of John's motives. That horrible day in the floral studio, Elizabeth had thought, now that the money was gone, John wanted to turn his back on her and her family.

But upon reflection, she could see that John had always been reluctant to take over the business. She'd brushed away his concerns every time he'd brought them up. No, John had been pure-hearted all along. It was she who'd been wrong.

**

Elizabeth joined her father in the breakfast room. Now that the fair was over, he'd resumed his more leisurely morning routine.

"I got the cable earlier this morning." Her father poured a spoonful of sugar into his coffee and stirred. "Mr. Banks was arrested last night. The police found him when he tried to cross the border into Canada at Niagara Falls. He had a suitcase full of money on him, and he'd attempted to disguise himself as a woman."

Elizabeth was glad the thief had been captured. "Does that mean we'll need to go back to New York now?"

"No, my lawyers will take care of everything. I might have to make a trip when it goes to trial, but that's a long time from now. We'll proceed as planned—only two more days until we leave for Seattle."

Her father got up and put another log in the fireplace. The breakfast room was warm and cozy. It was less grand than the other rooms in their apartment, but it was Elizabeth's favorite. It felt the most comfortable.

"Will we be living in a hotel for long once we get to Seattle?"

"I don't think so. We'll search for a house right away." Her father returned to his chair at the head of the table and studied his daughter for a moment. "I don't want to talk about Mr. Banks or Seattle right now. I want to talk about you and John. You've been evasive. What happened?"

Elizabeth sighed and played with the fringe on her napkin. "I'm sorry, Father. I know you wanted him to take over the business. It's your legacy. John doesn't think he's the right person to run an insurance business. I think I was pushing him into it."

"So, you called off the wedding? Elizabeth, I never wanted the business to be a burden. Not for you or the man you marry." He shook his head. "That was never my intention. If John doesn't want to take over the company, it's fine with me. I don't exactly understand what he does at that store, but I know he's good at his job. Marshall Field seems to consider John some kind of genius."

"I thought keeping the company in the family was important to you. It's important to me too. It was supposed to go to Samuel..."

"I don't think Samuel really wanted it. I made mistakes. I pushed him to be who I wanted him to be, and now all I want is to have him back. I was hard on your brother." He took a drink of coffee. "Elizabeth, you're not responsible for taking your brother's place. I hope you know that. The *company* is not my legacy. As we've seen, it can all disappear in the blink of an eye.

"I want to begin again in Seattle because I enjoy the challenge—and I'm not ready to retire yet. You and Samuel are my legacy. I'm proud of you, and I love you." Her father poured himself more coffee. "How are we going to fix this?"

Elizabeth had never heard her father speak like this before. His words touched her heart. "Fix it? I don't know. Forgiveness—will you forgive me? I've been seeking penance for my part in Samuel's death, but I don't think it's possible."

"Samuel's death was an accident, and I don't see anything to forgive, though I know you feel differently. You carry that guilt. And you're right

—it's not possible to absolve yourself. But you're not left to do it on your own. Jesus already did that for you. He's the one who has the power to forgive, and he extends that grace to all of us. We only need to accept it."

It was a truth that Elizabeth was finally ready to hear. Her father was right. She could spend the rest of her life trying to make up for Samuel's death, and it would never be enough—or she could accept God's forgiveness and grace and move on. She walked over to her father and hugged him. "Thank you."

"Now, about John...maybe you should go talk to him. And Elizabeth, if you want to marry him and stay in Chicago, you have my blessing. I should have told you that a long time ago."

***

John might be in the employee lunchroom. She'd check there first. After that long breakfast conversation with her father, Elizabeth was determined not to waste any more time leaving important matters unsaid. How John would choose to receive her apology wasn't in her control, but Elizabeth still owed him one. She left the Palmer House minutes after talking to her father, then walked to Marshall Field's.

It was already December, and winter was settling into the city. Elizabeth stepped carefully around an icy patch on the sidewalk as she approached the front entrance of the store. Even though it was cold, Elizabeth could feel perspiration dripping down the back of her tight corset. Her nervous energy was almost more than she could bear. *What if he won't even listen? He has every right to be angry with me.*

Mr. Macrillo, the doorman, smiled and greeted Elizabeth as she entered the store. Now that she was here, she felt foolish going into the employee lunchroom. Even as she walked past the glove counter, she could feel the stares from the salesladies. *Surely, they must know what I did.* Straightening her shoulders, she moved past them, pretending she didn't notice their judgmental glances.

Before Elizabeth climbed the store's grand staircase, she ran into Miss Andrews, the secretary who had introduced her to John on her very first day. She was glad because she wanted to say goodbye.

"Oh, hello, Miss Nordeman. I thought you'd already left for Seattle."

"Not yet, but soon. I just can't seem to stay away from this place." Elizabeth laughed, trying to hide the real purpose behind her visit. How much did Miss Andrews know about the breakup? "Have you seen Mr. Lewis around here somewhere?"

Miss Andrews looked confused. "He left a week ago."

"Oh, yes, of course..." Elizabeth felt like she had swallowed a sharp rock, and it was now sinking into her chest. "Well, actually—I didn't know. How might I reach him?"

"I thought he was going to Wisconsin to see his family—before the wedding."

Hadn't John told anyone the wedding was off? Had he quit his job? "You don't happen to know when he'll be back?" Elizabeth asked. She realized this probably sounded like a ridiculous question, coming from the man's fiancée.

"No, I'm sorry. I don't." The secretary's eyes looked like they were full of questions that she was too polite to ask.

"As you might already have guessed, the wedding was called off. It's okay. I'm glad I was able to see you before I left. Thank you for making me feel so welcome here."

But it wasn't okay. The small glimmer of hope that Elizabeth had been holding onto had been snuffed out. She quickly hugged Miss Andrews and left. All she wanted now was to go home, hide in her room, and cry.

CHAPTER TWENTY-SEVEN

John's brother, Horace, was waiting on the platform at the train station when John arrived in Belmont. His friendly face was a welcome sight. So was the familiar station. A white clapboard building stood alone next to the tracks. A light dusting of snow covered the vast prairie landscape. John was almost home. The men greeted each other with handshakes and some good-natured slaps on the back.

"Hey, how was the trip?" Horace asked.

"Just long enough. It feels good to stretch my legs. How's he doing?" John asked, referring to their father.

"He's resting. That's how we knew he was really sick. As you know, he doesn't like to ever stop moving. The doc says it's probably bronchitis. Mother is worried sick, but she was excited when I told her you were coming. You need some help with your luggage?"

John nodded. "Yes, thank you. There it is." John pointed to two large trunks on the edge of the platform. He packed his most treasured possessions and left the rest, hoping the next tenant might benefit from his generosity.

Horace's eyebrows shot up when he saw John's trunks. "Are both of those yours? How long are you staying?" he asked.

"I'm not sure yet." John didn't feel like explaining anything more.

"Well, it's good to see you, and of course, you're welcome to stay as long as you like."

The same day Elizabeth returned the ring and walked out on him, John received a telegram from Horace, telling him their father was very ill, and he should come soon—before it was too late. In a daze, feeling like everything he cared about was being ripped from him, John had gone to Mr. Field's office and told him there was a family emergency he needed to attend to. He was sorry, but he'd need to resign from his position at the store so he could return to Wisconsin.

It was a terrible time of year to leave the store, since Christmas was only a couple of weeks away, and John didn't want to let his boss down, but he didn't see a choice in the matter. He expected the man would be angry—and he was. But then, Mr. Field had told him to not make a hasty decision, and he'd promised to keep John's position open as long as possible. It was a moment of grace on an otherwise awful day.

John followed his brother to the wagon. He greeted Lucy and Tom, the family's old draft horses, with scratches on their muzzles, and then they loaded his trunks into the back. After climbing up to the driver's seat, next to his brother, they settled in for the last hour of travel to the farm.

"How's Mary?" John asked.

Horace smiled. "She's great. You're going to get another little niece or nephew very soon."

"Is that so?" John felt a twinge of jealousy for a brief moment. He wondered if he'd ever have children of his own. "Well, I'll be. That's exciting!"

"Mother is delighted to get to see you, and don't get me wrong, but I think she's even more excited to meet Elizabeth, and so is Alice. She'll probably be at the house when we get there. Have you two set a date for the wedding?"

There it was. John had been dreading that question. "There isn't going to be a wedding."

Horace was quiet for a long moment. "I'm sorry to hear it, Brother."

John was grateful that Horace didn't press for more information. They were quiet for the next several minutes. The dirt roads were frozen, making for a bumpy ride. Even so, John nearly fell asleep as the wagon made its way past familiar farmhouses, barns, and fields. Over the past couple of days, he'd barely slept. But now, John felt the tension he'd been carrying around slowly release as the wagon brought him closer to home.

Their dog, Jack, greeted John when Horace pulled back the reins and stopped the wagon in front of the house. The white Lab barked excitedly and wagged his tail as the men climbed down from the wagon. Their sister, Alice, came out of the house onto the front porch, followed by her daughter.

John's niece ran down the front steps and into his arms. "Uncle John!"

"Ida! How are you, sweet girl? I heard you had a birthday recently—but you don't look a day over ten," John teased.

Ida had been telling anyone who asked that she was ten, for several years now. John understood it was wishful thinking—mostly having to do with the fact that she wanted to be able to keep up with her older brothers. The fourteen-year-old twins, Elijah and Don, occasionally included their younger sister in their activities—but not nearly enough for Ida's liking.

"Uncle John, don't tell anyone, but I'm actually eight," Ida whispered.

"Ah, well, that's okay. I have a present for you, anyway." John reached into his pocket and pulled out a silver dollar, then he handed it to Ida.

Ida's eyes sparkled and her mouth dropped open. "Thank you!"

Soon, the whole family—minus Alvertus, the patriarch—surrounded the weary traveler. After a round of hugs and warm greetings, everyone made their way into the house.

"Can I see him now?" John asked.

His mother, Myrtle, nodded as she took his coat, hat, and gloves. "Yes, he's in his room. Go on. He'll be happy to see you."

The older man was asleep when John went in, so he sat next to the bed in a rocking chair and waited. John didn't want to wake him, and he needed to sit quietly for a minute to gather his thoughts. It was disconcerting to see his father, a man who'd always been a steady, strong, presence in his life, asleep in the middle of the day. He appeared smaller now.

John shut his eyes and prayed, *Oh, Jesus, healer of the sick, you know what it's like to endure pain. Look kindly upon my father today and restore his health. Amen.*

John listened to his father's raspy breaths for a while, until finally, he began coughing. The coughing fit caused him to wake up. When he did, John helped him sit up, then handed him a glass of water that was sitting on the nightstand.

In spite of the obvious discomfort he was in, John's father managed a smile. "Hey, Son—"

"Hey, Pops. It's good to see you—"

***

The next day, John was in the barn, feeding the horses, when Stuart Peterson showed up. Mary's brother had settled into the old cabin on the backside of the family's property. He'd been helping Horace with the farm.

"Hey, there, old friend!" John held out his hand to greet Stuart. "How's country life treating you?"

Stuart shook John's hand and grinned. "Not bad. Your family has been so welcoming. They've made me feel right at home here."

John smiled but didn't say anything. Horace had already told him last night that not only was Stuart doing a lot of work on the farm, but he'd also been going to town regularly. Alice lived in town. Stuart told Horace that he was just helping out a single mother with some chores around her house. Never mind that Alice already had two strong teen-age sons who helped with those things. And whenever their sister was visiting the house, Stuart had a way of showing up soon after. Neither Stuart nor Alice had said anything to the family yet. But according to Horace, judging from the way those two looked at each other, they were clearly in love. John was happy for them.

"Do you have time to go for a ride this morning?" John asked Stuart. "Maybe Horace would want to come too."

"Sure. I just need to finish raking out these stalls first. Then I can go."

John went into the house to ask Horace if he wanted to come along. When he entered the kitchen, he was pleased to find his father sitting at the breakfast table, drinking his coffee. John's mother was standing in front of the stove, cooking bacon. Only yesterday, the man had barely been able to sit up, and his skin had appeared gray. Today, his father seemed more like himself.

Did you have breakfast yet? Sit down," the elder Mr. Lewis said.

"Mary made me some breakfast, earlier, but I'll have another cup of coffee with you. You're looking better."

"I *feel* better. The doc was overreacting, I'm sure. I'm going to be fine." His father leaned back in his chair and eyed John. "Horace tells me the wedding is off. What happened?" The man was direct, as always.

"She's moving to Seattle with her family."

"You were willing to move to New York with her. New York—Seattle—as long as you're together, what's the difference? Can't say I'd want to live in either of those places, but as we all know, you belong in the city."

"I'd have gone to Seattle. I know it's important for Elizabeth to be near her family, but I told her I didn't want to take over her father's insurance business. I'm good at what I do, in retail. I enjoy it. As much as I tried to convince myself that I could do it, for her, it wasn't in me. I'm the wrong person for the job." John wished what he was saying wasn't true. "I'd run that business into the ground in no time. I didn't want to be the cause of something like that. I should have told her the truth a long time ago. When I finally did tell her, I had terrible timing. It's a long story, but the short end of it is, she must have thought I was only marrying her for her fortune—which is the farthest thing from the truth. She gave me back her engagement ring. I never got to explain."

"And now you're here." His father took a bite of his eggs. "If you weren't going to work for her father in Seattle, what would you have done instead?"

"I'd hoped I could work for another department store and do what I did for Marshall Field's."

"And what was that?"

John proceeded to tell his father about the store's expansion, the window displays, the wedding dress he'd designed, and many other ideas he'd implemented at the store over the past year. His father listened politely, but John could tell he didn't really understand John's role or accomplishments.

Stuart wandered into the kitchen and listened to the conversation for a minute. "Your son is being modest, sir," he said, interrupting the conversation. "He won't tell you this, so I will. He's so good at his job that the big department stores in New York City often send their employees to Marshall Field's so they can learn from the best and copy his ideas. The window displays he creates often draw large crowds on the street outside."

John, who was feeling embarrassed now, stood from the table and cleared his throat. He looked at Stuart. "Are you ready to go on that ride?"

"Sure. Is Horace coming?"

"Horace went to fetch the midwife," John's mother said from where she stood at the stove. "It's time for the baby to come. Alice is upstairs with Mary right now." John's mother had been quiet during the conversation, but he realized she'd been listening the whole time. "Go on, take some apples and cheese with you."

"John," his father called.

"Yes?"

His father glanced down before meeting John's gaze directly. "I'm proud of you, Son."

John had never heard his father say those words to him. He smiled and nodded. "Thank you."

John's life might be a mess right now, but at that moment, he knew he would be okay.

***

Horace and Mary named their newborn girl Eunice. Both mother and baby were healthy, and Horace was over the moon with happiness. John smiled and said a silent prayer of thanks as he watched his mother rocking her grandbaby near the woodstove in the sitting room.

He was too young to remember when Horace was a baby, but John could remember his mother rocking Alice in that same chair. His mother loved babies, and she seemed content as she hummed and stroked Eunice's soft cheek.

His father was dozing in the chair opposite his wife. It was a cozy scene.

John couldn't believe it had only been a week since he'd come home. His father was continuing to look healthier every day, and the ugly cough had all but disappeared. It didn't escape John's notice that the original reason he'd come —to say his final goodbye to his father—had been replaced with a different, much happier purpose. His father had been granted a miracle with his recovery. And now, they'd welcomed a new precious life into the family.

John put down his book and gazed out the window toward the barn. It was getting dark outside—probably time to help Horace and Stuart with the chores.

"They'll get along fine without you, John," his mother said, seeming to read his thoughts.

He knew she was referring to more than the evening chores, and she was right. He'd enjoyed seeing his family, and they were nothing but welcoming, but it was clear to everyone that the farm wasn't the place where John belonged—no more than the insurance office had been. John missed his work at the store.

Elizabeth had been haunting his thoughts, too, but he believed that chapter of his life was over—and the sooner he learned to accept it, the better. "I think I'd better get back to Chicago soon, before I'm out of a job," John said to his mother.

"Chicago? I was hoping you'd say Seattle."

It was a selfless statement, because without a doubt, his mother would have preferred having him closer to home. She'd supported him when he'd first gone to Chicago, years ago, telling him to pursue his art, even though John recognized it had been hard for her—and that was only one day's travel from the farm by train.

"Are you trying to send me away as far as you can?" John teased, but he was deflecting.

"It seems to me that if there has been a misunderstanding between you and Elizabeth, you ought to make it right."

"I meant it when I said I didn't want to take over her father's business. I haven't changed my mind. There isn't a misunderstanding."

"I wasn't talking about that. You were right to speak up if you didn't want to run the Nordeman's family's business, but I think you know what I mean. I'm sure she would understand... if you only explained." She paused. "You'll stay for Christmas, won't you? It's only a couple more days."

John smiled. "Yes, I'll stay for Christmas."

Eunice started fussing, so John's mother stood to take the baby back to the bedroom where Mary was resting, leaving her son alone with his thoughts. John understood what his mother wanted him to do, and the reason why—and while he appreciated that she wanted him to be happy, he also knew that she didn't have the whole story.

Even if John explained what he'd meant, and Elizabeth did want to marry him—and she'd made it clear, she didn't—how could he reasonably expect to take care of her in the style she was accustomed to? John didn't have those kinds of resources. Not unless he worked for her father. No, John needed to be realistic. He'd go back to Chicago, swallow his pride, and resume his work at the store.

It would be necessary to find a new place to live when he got there. John was sorry he'd given up his apartment. A job and a place to lay his head at night was all he needed. That's what he told himself, anyway.

***

The day after Christmas, a mudslide took out a portion of the train tracks between Chicago and Belmont, causing a delay for several more days. Those extra days only made John more anxious to return to the store. He'd never taken so much time off from working before.

After arriving in Chicago, late Tuesday night, John checked into a cheap hotel. Instead of sleeping, he lay all night on his back, staring at the dirty, smoked-stained ceiling, silently willing the minutes to pass. All he wanted was to go back to work and have everything return to the way it had been—*before* he'd hired Miss Nordeman.

John stopped to hang his overcoat in his office when he got to the store on Wednesday morning, but the door was locked. Since he'd never secured it before, he wasn't even sure if he had a key. None John had with him worked.

I'll sort this out later—after I speak with Mr. Field.

John continued down the hallway, holding his coat over his right arm. He knocked on Mr. Field's door and waited a moment before entering.

His boss jumped forward in his chair when he saw John. "How was your trip?"

"It was good, thank you." John hesitated. "I wasn't in my right mind when I spoke with you last, and I appreciate the way you saved me from being too hasty. I'm back now and ready to get to work. What do you have for me?"

Mr. Field took a cigar box out of his top drawer and offered one to John. When he declined, Mr. Field took one for himself and lit the end. "We find ourselves in a bit of a predicament, then. You've been replaced. I didn't think you were coming back."

CHAPTER TWENTY-EIGHT

W hen Elizabeth left Union Station, five days before Christmas, she did so with tears in her eyes. Before she boarded the train, she gave Sissy, her maid, and Louis, the family's coachman, one last hug. They were both going back to New York to be closer to their families. Only their housekeeper, Annette, would be going to Seattle with the Nordemans,

This would be the Nordeman's final trip using their private Pullman car. Mr. Nordeman had found a buyer for the car on the west coast. Elizabeth understood, and even supported, her father's decision to liquidate many of the family's more extravagant luxuries, but that didn't mean it was any easier to see them go. At least she'd be able to enjoy this three-day journey in comfort.

Elizabeth sat on a plush green velvet sofa across from her mother, who was reading quietly. Her father was currently nearby in the barber's chair, fully reclined, with a hot towel covering his face. The barber, who was actually a multi-talented porter, had just given her father a shave. They were traveling through Wisconsin right now, according to the talkative barber. Elizabeth thought about John and the stories he'd told her about growing up on his farm in this state. It made her sad to think she would likely never see him again.

Elizabeth didn't know what to expect when they arrived in Seattle. All she knew was what she'd heard from her father. It was not a large city, and the population was still recovering from a devastating fire that had destroyed much of it a few years before. The port city's landscape included lots of trees and mountains. That was about all he'd told her.

Elizabeth realized her father saw significant opportunities for growth with his new insurance company, and she enjoyed seeing how excited he was when he talked about the challenges in front of him. She marveled at how the prospect of starting all over again had reinvigorated her father, instead of discouraging him. He seemed like a new, younger version of the man he'd been only a year ago.

In the past few weeks, Elizabeth had begun to notice that her father was more willing to talk about his profession with her than he'd been in the past—and sometimes he would even solicit her ideas. She wasn't sure if this was simply because she was readily available, or because he'd begun to see her as someone who had a good head for business. She wanted to believe it was the latter. Elizabeth's hope that her father would relent on some of his old-fashioned ideas about women was rekindled. Now that she was no longer getting married, would he consider letting her have a place in the new company?

Elizabeth watched from the window inside the car as the train sped along through the vast snow-covered prairie. There wasn't much to look at, so she pulled out the letter she'd been working on for several days now. It was for John.

Unsure of what to say, she'd thrown away several earlier attempts, but Elizabeth knew she needed to at least try to convey how sorry she felt for how she'd ended their engagement. He was owed that much. Elizabeth figured she could address the letter to John in care of Marshall Field's.

Even if he was still away from the store, he'd get it eventually. They'd know where to forward the letter. All she needed to do was finish writing it, give it to the conductor, and have it sent along at the next train stop. .

The barber was cleaning his tools now. Father was sitting upright again, appearing remarkably relaxed for a man who'd just had a sharp blade to his throat while hurtling sixty miles per hour down steel tracks. He thanked the man and turned his attention to Elizabeth and his wife. "Should I order some tea and cake?"

"Yes—please. Come sit over here," Elizabeth said.

Now seemed as good a time as ever to ask if she could work for him. Elizabeth had her father's undivided attention, he was in a good mood, and the words she wanted to say had been well-rehearsed in her mind.

After her father ordered the tea, he settled into a wingback chair near Elizabeth. He pointed toward the letter she had in front of her. "What are you working on there?"

"Oh, it's nothing," Elizabeth replied, putting it away. "Well...actually, to tell you the truth, it's an apology letter to John. I'm not even sure where to send it—or if it will ever reach him, but I'm going to try. I put a lot of pressure on him to take over the business, and it wasn't fair of me to do that." She paused. "But I want to ask you something, and it's really important to me. Would you please consider allowing me to work with you? I want to learn, and I believe I could do a good job. My floral business turned a profit right from the start, and I enjoyed doing it."

Elizabeth watched her parents' faces as she waited for an answer. Neither one of them looked as surprised by her request as she had expected.

Her father smiled. "I've been thinking the same thing. I was going to ask if you'd be interested in helping me set up the office once we get to Seattle. Yes, I think we'll make a great team. Don't you agree, Patricia?"

Her mother smiled. "I do—but don't think I've changed my mind about wanting to see you married soon, Elizabeth. A young woman gets to a certain age, and let's just say, her options become more limited. I don't want that for you, dear. Send that letter. I've always liked John."

Elizabeth smiled, nodded, and took a bite of the chocolate cake the train attendant put on the table in front of her. She didn't expect sending the letter would change anything. If she couldn't marry John, Elizabeth would rather be an old spinster—but now, at least she'd have some interesting work she could pour herself into—though she'd never voice that thought out-loud to her mother.

***

Upon arriving in Seattle, the Nordeman family checked into the Diller Hotel, which was in a new brick building downtown. It wasn't fancy, but it had running water, toilets, and a working elevator—more than what could be said of their other choices.

The concierge at the front desk offered to personally show the Nordeman's around the city after finding out they were new to Seattle and searching for a house. He was a friendly older man with a white beard and round spectacles. He introduced himself as Mr. Parker.

"You're the only guests we have right now, so instead of twiddling my thumbs here, inside, I might as well make myself useful," he said.

Elizabeth's father said they would be happy to take Mr. Parker up on his offer. Even though they were only two days away from Christmas, the mild outside temperatures and sunshine felt inviting.

The only snow Elizabeth could see was far away, covering the mountains in the distance. A warm December was a change—different from Chicago and New York—that Elizabeth could readily embrace. She followed along with her mother, father, and Mr. Parker as they walked along First Avenue.

"That's the Denny Hotel up there—it's not finished yet. They call it the 'ghost palace,'" Mr. Parker said, pointing to a massive building at the top of a hill.

For all its grandeur, it had an unsettling quality, and its nickname seemed appropriate. Seattle, like much of the rest of the country, was suffering from some severe economic woes.

"This whole area had to be rebuilt after the fire," Mr. Parker explained. "And everything was going well, up until this spring. Since then, a lot of the construction has been put to a halt. Many of these buildings are empty. Bankruptcies, layoffs, what have you—it's tough right now for a lot of people, but we'll spring back. If you're seeking to invest in property, now's a perfect time."

Elizabeth listened to Mr. Parker and her father talk back and forth as they walked up a steep hill. There were a lot of hills in this city. Though a bit rough around the edges, it was a beautiful place. They made a right turn at the next corner, onto a residential street with pretty Colonial Revival style homes.

The concierge pointed to a large white house across the street. "That one belongs to my boss. It's empty, and I happen to know he's interested in selling it."

"It's lovely," Elizabeth said.

Her mother nodded. "Yes—it is."

Elizabeth could hear the longing in her mother's voice. Elizabeth understood. The thought of how disappointing it must have been for her mother, to pour so much effort into having their home in New York rebuilt after the fire, only to have it taken away, pained Elizabeth deeply. She knew her father felt the same way. Having a home to call their own was what they all wanted.

***

On Christmas morning, her father told Elizabeth and her mother to get dressed for a walk outside, because he had a special surprise for them. He led them straight to the house they'd admired a couple of days ago.

"Last night was your final night in a hotel for a long while—because this is our home now." He gestured toward the white house. "I bought it yesterday, and it's ready for us to move in. Merry Christmas!"

Elizabeth's father pulled a key from his pocket and handed it to her mother, who began crying. Then she kissed him. "Don't worry, these are happy tears. Thank you."

What Elizabeth loved most about that moment was the expression of pride and the apparent joy that her father took in giving this gift to her mother. She was delighted for them. But

Elizabeth discreetly wiped away her tears. She didn't want to spoil her parent's special moment. But all she could think about was how John had once tried to buy a house for her—and she'd ruined everything.

CHAPTER TWENTY-NINE

Mr. Field let out a puff of smoke and looked across his desk. John remained quiet and waited for his boss to say more. The man appeared to be thinking. "I moved Mrs. Sanders and Miss Walsh out of the alterations department while you were gone and had them take over your duties. Miss Walsh has been taking care of the floral arrangements. They're a good team—fine work. The ladies asked if they could continue permanently in their new roles if you didn't come back, and I said yes. Just yesterday, I told them they were the new joint directors of visual merchandising. But if you want your old job back, you can tell them. We'll send them back to alterations."

John didn't know what to say. He didn't want to do that to the women. "I appreciate that, sir— but maybe there's a way the ladies can continue working in visual merchandising."

"This is a business, Mr. Lewis, not a charity. What do you propose?"

"I'm not sure—"

"As I said, it's a predicament. Figure it out— and soon. But while you're here, I have another question for you. Is it true that you and Elizabeth Nordeman called off the wedding?"

"It's true, sir."

"And why is that?"

John did not want to be having this conversation. But Mr. Field had acted as an advisor of sorts from the beginning of his courtship with Elizabeth. It was a fair question. John eventually told his mentor everything. When he finished speaking, Mr. Field looked thoughtful.

"I hate to lose a good employee, but you need to leave. Go to Seattle. Win her back!"

It was the same advice his mother had given him. Maybe they were right. But was it a risk worth taking?

"I know a man in Seattle, a Swede named Mr. Nelson. He's part owner of a store called Frederick and Nelson. I believe his goal for the store is to make it as great as Marshall Field's. As long as he stays in Seattle, I'm fine with that. Tell him I sent you. If he's smart—and I think he is—he'll hire you."

John's heart felt like it was in his throat. He fiddled with the diamond ring that was still in his pocket. He understood, once he said the words out loud, he wouldn't be able to take them back—not this time.

"Mr. Field, I'm grateful for the opportunities you've given me over the years. You've been a great teacher and boss, and I've learned from the best. Thank you for everything. Mrs. Sanders and Miss Walsh both deserve to continue where they are. I'm going to go to Seattle. Respectfully, I want to tender my resignation as of today."

Mr. Field nodded and shook John's hand. "I wish you all the best, Mr. Lewis."

John would miss this store, and his future was full of questions, but it didn't matter. John finally had clarity on what was best for him.

On his way out, John stopped by Miss Andrew's desk to say goodbye, though he didn't explain why. The secretary stood and came over to where he was standing, offering a handshake. "Wait," she said. "I have some mail for you." After handing over several envelopes wrapped in twine, her face took on a somber expression. "Miss Nordeman came here, searching for you while you were away. Are you going to Seattle?"

John was surprised by the question. How much did she know? "Yes—"

"Perfect. You're a good man, John. I'll miss seeing you around, but you're doing the right thing.

Minutes later, on the street outside Marshall Field's, John stopped to admire a new window display. It must have been done by Miss Walsh and Mrs. Sanders. He was genuinely happy for them—and hoped they'd enjoy the job as much as he had. Then John remembered to look through the letters Miss Andrews had given him.

He saw Elizabeth's handwriting on the front of one, and his pulse quickened. Ripping open the envelope, John quickly scanned the letter. He'd take his time reading later. For now, he needed to know the answer to one question— would she be willing to give him another chance?

It was a short but apologetic letter, but Elizabeth's words offered John a glimmer of hope. He caught a whiff of her perfume on the thick paper—lily of the valley. He smiled when he saw she'd left an address for the hotel where she'd be staying. It was enough.

**

On January 3, 1894, John arrived in Seattle tired but determined. Today was the beginning of a new life—and he had every intention of sharing that life with Elizabeth. It was a bright, cold day. Mount Rainier, like a majestic white queen, standing alone, dominated the view to the south. To the west, stood the snow-capped peaks of the Olympics.

John found a Hansom cab outside the train depot. He told the driver to take him to a hotel. As the cab drew closer to downtown, John could see the sparkling blue expanse of Elliot Bay ahead. Many of the buildings appeared newly built. Seattle was a logging and fishing town. The air smelled like freshly cut timber and saltwater. The city was larger than John had expected. Overall, it was a beautiful place, and it seemed to be full of possibilities. Optimism filled John's spirit.

The cab stopped in front of a tidy brick building on First Street, and John recognized the name on the sign as the place where Elizabeth said she'd be staying—The Diller Hotel. It was too soon.

"I prefer a different hotel, sir," John told the driver. Though he wanted nothing more than to see Elizabeth right now, his best course of action would be to wait. She was so close, and the thought of seeing her again had propelled him forward to this point—but first, he needed a job.

It was still early in the day. After the cab dropped John off at Hotel Seattle, John wasted no time. He washed up, put on a fresh suit, and headed back outside to find the store Mr. Field had mentioned—Frederick and Nelson.

"We're not hiring right now." Mr. Nelson said after John explained the purpose behind his visit.

John took a deep breath and prayed a silent prayer. He'd come too far to meet with failure now. *God, I ask for your favor right now...*

CHAPTER THIRTY

"We need some furniture for this office," Elizabeth said, surveying the storefront.

"I'll put you in charge of that." Her father laid his hand on her shoulder. "Start a list. Take some measurements. We'll go to Frederick and Nelson this afternoon and see if they have what we need."

The building was small, but it was only a few blocks from their home, and it would do for now. Elizabeth's father pulled out his key and opened the front door. The bare space was cold and empty but full of possibilities. Elizabeth was prepared. She took a measuring tape, a notebook, and a pen from the leather satchel she carried and got to work.

After an hour of exploring their new place and making plans, Father and Elizabeth took a streetcar to Frederick and Nelson. Upon entering the store, Elizabeth looked around with appreciation. An impressive variety of finely made furniture filled the store. Not bad for a small city so far out west. She wandered over to take a closer inspection of a large mahogany desk.

"Think big, Elizabeth. We'll need at least four desks to start," her father said before walking away to check out the lamps on the next floor.

The young salesman, who had been coming over to greet them, overheard her father's words —and the look on his face changed from one of mild interest to fawning enthusiasm. "Hello, miss. May I help you with anything today?"

"Yes, I like this desk. I was wondering..." Her words trailed off.

Across the room, two well-dressed men were quietly speaking and pointing to a shelf. Their backs were turned toward Elizabeth, so she couldn't see their faces, but there was something familiar about the taller man. It couldn't be. Was it? She held her breath as she waited to see if he would turn so she could see his face.

"Is everything okay, miss?" the salesman asked.

"Yes—I thought I recognized someone. Sorry."

"That's Mr. Nelson over there."

"And the other man?"

Elizabeth didn't need to wait for an answer. At that moment, the men turned around. John! He seemed to notice her at the same time. His jaw dropped open, then a huge smile came over his face. *Oh, how I've missed that smile.*

"Oh, that's Mr. Lewis," the salesman said. "He's our new guy—just moved here from Chicago."

Forgetting everything else, Elizabeth moved toward John, as though being pulled by a magnet. It took all her self-control to keep from running toward him and wrapping her arms around his neck.

"I should have guessed I'd find you here." His voice carried a hint of a tease, mixed with affection.

"John? You work here?"

"I do." Then, as if remembering where he was, John quickly regained his composure. "Miss Nordeman, this is Mr. Nelson, the owner of this store and my boss. Mr. Nelson, Miss Nordeman recently relocated from Chicago like me. We..." John smiled. "We used to work together."

While Elizabeth and Mr. Nelson were exchanging greetings, her father came back downstairs. When he saw John, he seemed momentarily taken aback and just as shocked as Elizabeth had been, but after recovering, he offered a handshake and a warm smile.

It was an awkward exchange. There were so many questions Elizabeth wanted to ask, but they all would have been inappropriate at the moment.

Her father, as if sensing his daughter's plight, quietly scribbled their new address on an old business card and handed it to John. "Here's our address. Come by after you're finished working tonight. Dinner is at seven."

John nodded and slipped the card into his pocket. "Thank you, sir. I'll be there."

***

Elizabeth and her father were sitting by the fireplace reading. It was a scene of domestic tranquility that belied the inner commotion she was doing her best to conceal. After that morning's unexpected surprise with John, Elizabeth's mind had been in a fog. She'd re-read the first sentence in her novel multiple times, but the words on the page might as well have been written in a foreign language.

Anyway, the book was merely a prop to hide behind—an effort to avoid conversation. The hope that, maybe, she could have a second chance with John had been sparked. Why else would John have come to Seattle? But like a spark that could be easily smothered, she wanted to protect it. At this point, talking about why John was in Seattle and why he was coming for dinner seemed too risky. Questions remained. Why didn't he tell her he was there?

The doorbell chimed. Shortly after, Annette showed John into the front sitting room. Dinner wouldn't be served for another hour, but Elizabeth was glad he was early. The waiting had been agony.

"Good evening, John," her father said, standing to greet their guest. "It's good to see you again." He spoke as if everything about this strange moment was perfectly normal. "If you'll excuse me, I'll leave you two to talk." He took a quick leave and went upstairs to join Elizabeth's mother, who was still dressing for dinner.

John, who was now alone with Elizabeth, gave her a sheepish grin. "I received your letter. Thank you. And I know, coming out here was incredibly presumptuous. But—"

"I'm happy you came—and I'm so sorry for the way I reacted when you said you didn't want to work for my father. I wish I could take it back. Will you forgive me?"

John didn't say anything. Instead, he pulled Elizabeth into his arms, then he reached down and kissed her. Elizabeth kissed him in return with every bit of passion she'd been holding back for too long. Before they separated, he whispered, "There's nothing to forgive."

It was a generous statement, and Elizabeth felt undeserving of such a gift, but she was learning to accept the grace that God and others offered to her without question. "I was hoping you'd come after me."

"I should have, right away. That same day, I left to see my family. My father was very ill. He's better now, but I haven't stopped thinking about you. I was waiting to get a job here before I contacted you. I didn't want to come to you empty-handed. Mr. Nelson hired me this morning. Minutes later, you appeared—an answered prayer." John smiled.

"Congratulations on the new job. I have one too. I'll be taking over the insurance business once I've learned the ropes."

"I always thought you were perfect for that role." John looked genuinely happy for her. "I've been carrying something that belongs to you in my pocket for the past few weeks, and I was wondering if you wanted it back?" He took out the ring.

"Yes!" Elizabeth grinned as she held her left hand out for John to put the ring back where it belonged.

Acknowledgments

There are many gracious people who have contributed in this book's journey toward publication. Tara, my first beta reader, Jessica and Amanda, my critique partners--thank you--for helping me with this story. I owe each of you a huge debt of gratitude. You bless me. I also want to thank my wonderful editor, who teaches, encourages, and pushes me in a good way. And of course, my family...Derek, Grace, Trent--I love you.

ABOUT THE AUTHOR

Dawn Klinge is a Pacific Northwest native who loves a rainy day, a hot cup of coffee, and a good book to get lost in. This wife and mom to two young adults is often inspired by true personal and historical accounts. Dawn is a member of the American Christian Fiction Writers Association. Her other books in the Historic Hotels Collection are Sorrento Girl and Biltmore Girl (coming Spring 2021).

www.dawnklinge.com

Made in the USA
Monee, IL
25 June 2021

72315383R10174